Joanna Harrison

A Northern Lily

five years of an uneventful life - Vol. 3

Joanna Harrison

A Northern Lily
five years of an uneventful life - Vol. 3

ISBN/EAN: 9783337850883

Printed in Europe, USA, Canada, Australia, Japan

Cover: Foto ©Andreas Hilbeck / pixelio.de

More available books at **www.hansebooks.com**

Five Years of an Uneventful Life

BY

JOANNA HARRISON

VOL. III.

CHAPTER VIII.

' I have built
Two chauntries, where the sad and solemn priests
Sing still for Richard's soul.   More will I do ;
Though all that I can do is nothing worth,
Since that my penitence comes after call,
Imploring pardon.'

ELSIE remained at Alkerton for many weeks;
her presence became almost a necessity to
Lady Eleanor, who talked to her as she did
to no one else, and regarded her with a
great deal more affection, probably, than if
Elsie had really been her daughter-in-law.
The companionship was good for both, and
gave Elsie in particular an interest in life.
Hers was a nature which required some one
to cherish and take care of, and she became
passionately attached to David's mother, who
confided in her, and leant upon her ; speaking
when they were alone as unreservedly as if

Elsie had been a woman of her own age. She traced the whole course of David's childhood and youth from the day of his birth, dwelling more particularly on the time when he first began to walk, 'when every one who came to the house admired him,' and she showed Elsie a collection of little soft curls of hair, cut from her children's heads at various stages of their life. Then David's schoolboy letters were brought out, and dwelt upon one by one; most of those he had written latterly she had not kept, which she regretted now with tears. Sometimes, but rarely, she had fits of remorse, when she said she had been unjust to David, and which it required all Elsie's skill to soothe; but it made her almost happy again to hear how her boy had loved and admired her, and how often he had spoken to Elsie of his mother.

'Oh, Elsie! it is so hard that he should have been the one to be taken from me. I never dreamt of it, never. We always said David was so lucky; I never was anxious about him because of that.   He never gave me a moment's anxiety since he was born.   But I was so proud of him, and I used to hope and plan things for him'—she stopped to wipe away the tears which were running down her face—'I was so sure he would distinguish himself.   But oh, if I had known there would be fighting, I would never —never have let him go into the army.'

'Dear Lady Eleanor, we should not grudge him,' said Elsie earnestly, laying her hand upon her friend's knee.   'I do not. He was a soldier, you know, and he—he did his duty.   What would become of the country if everybody kept back their sons?'

'I don't see how his being killed does the country the least good,' said Lady Eleanor disconsolately, 'and what is the use of people distinguishing themselves, and having medals and things if they are dead?   I would not let Lionel enter one of those dangerous professions for anything in the world.   Though Lionel is not David'—she ended with a heavy sigh—'*he* never got into scrapes.'

'Is Lionel not—not doing well at Oxford, then?'

'Ah well, I have had a great deal of trouble with him altogether. He has left Oxford now—you did not know that, by the bye—and his bills keep coming in, and that annoys Frederick so. He can't bear paying bills—though Lionel's debts are not very bad ones, poor boy. I wish sometimes he would come back.'

'Where is he, then?' asked Elsie, 'since he has left Oxford?'

'He is still wandering about abroad,' said Lady Eleanor. 'He is at Vienna now, and talks of Paris as his next address—that looks as if he were on his way home, doesn't it?'

'Yes, certainly, I should say. Then he has been making a tour abroad?'

'It was Frederick's doing,' said Lady Eleanor wearily; 'he said he would not have him idling at home. You see Lionel was plucked—and then his debts—and he certainly spoke very improperly to Frederick. But I wish he was at home again.'

'Is he working at anything?' asked Elsie.

'Oh yes, music. He has a passion for music, you know. He goes to all the operas he can—he says he wants to form his taste, and would take lessons if he could find any one fit to teach him. I wonder he can have the heart to play on the piano.'

It was curious how Elsie could put aside her own grief to comfort David's mother, and behaved as if the loss had not fallen so heavily upon herself. She now began to question her more particularly concerning Lionel, partly in order to divert her mind from her worst trouble, partly because she herself was anxious to have news of her former friend and playfellow. Lady Eleanor was always ready to talk of Lionel, and the loss of her younger son would really have been a far more crushing grief to her than that of David. Lionel had been idle and extravagant; no more serious faults could be imputed to him. He had a refined nature and tastes, which led him to avoid low associates, and to detest the grosser forms of dissipation. But he had given quite sufficient annoyance to his parents by his incorrigible idleness, although in some respects they misunderstood him. He had been excessively shocked and grieved at his brother's death, and had honestly set himself to work in order to make up to his mother in some measure for what she had lost. But he had let too much time slip away before, and though he worked his hardest for the few weeks he had left before his next examination, he was plucked, to his own disappointment, and the indignation of his parents, who now reproached him with being heartless and unfeeling as well as idle. This was too much for Lionel's temper to stand, and high words passed between him and his stepfather; the upshot of which was, that Lionel left home, rather under a cloud, to pursue his so-called musical studies abroad. There, having no particular inducement to work, and thinking himself rather hardly used by both parents, he relapsed somewhat into his former idle ways, although his character had gained in manliness and gravity since David's death.

Lady Eleanor did not see or know all this, but Elsie partly divined it from the story she told, and felt sorry for Lionel, whom she always judged leniently. She tried to impress his mother with her view of the case, and Lady Eleanor was very ready to listen to her, and would bring up the subject over and over again for the sake of having it repeated; until they both persuaded themselves that Lionel was an injured martyr, deserving of the tenderest and most respectful treatment. It was well for Lady Eleanor's happiness that she had taken up this idea; for she had greatly added to her burden of sorrow by trying, however unsuccessfully, to harden her heart against her remaining son. She now wrote affectionately, urging him to come home; and Mr. Fitzgerald, to please his wife, consented to overlook all hasty expressions on Lionel's part, on condition that the latter ceased to expect him to keep hunters for him, or to pay any more of his debts.

Lionel accordingly returned to Alkerton a little before Christmas. His coming cheered up the household, though at first he was unlike the Lionel of old times, grave and sometimes low-spirited. He treated Elsie with a sort of tender reverence, and was exceedingly thoughtful for her comfort; at first indeed he hardly dared to speak to her, but watched her from afar with wistful admiring eyes. By degrees he became more familiar; and when Elsie talked to him and tried to draw him out, he gave her his confidence very fully. He knew he was an idle dog, he would say, and good for nothing, he had got into the habit of it. He would go out to Australia, that was the only thing he was fit for. This was in his most desponding moods, which gradually became rarer, as his walks and talks with Elsie were more frequent. He had another scheme for his more cheerful hours. He would go to Ardvoira and live there, when the present tenant's lease had expired; build cottages, and improve the condition of his tenantry; and keep a steam-yacht. Neither

would he listen to any nonsense from his
tenants (mind you); but they, under his
judicious and paternal rule, would become so
intelligent that they would in time refrain from
making any idiotic suggestions about reduc-
tions of rent or undue burnings of heather.

To all this Elsie listened and smiled; she
favoured the Ardvoira scheme more than
the Australian one, but she knew that his
mother really did not know what to do with
the boy, and that she and Mr. Fitzgerald
had some new plan for him every day. Lady
Eleanor was now fairly cheerful again, and
seldom spoke of David, unless it were to
allude to his untimely death as a reason for
keeping Lionel out of any possible danger.
Mr. Fitzgerald proposed that his stepson
should travel for a year or two, and this
Elsie too thought rather a sensible suggestion, but Lady Eleanor would not hear of it.
She watched Lionel's evident devotion to
Elsie with favour, and contrived to take
credit to herself for thinking that she would
not throw obstacles in the way of her child's

happiness, and that if he chose to fall in love
with Elsie, she would not oppose it, or seek
out a more worldly match for him. To be
sure Elsie evidently looked upon him as a
mere boy, but that, Lady Eleanor argued
with herself, was very ridiculous, and she
would soon find out her mistake, for Lionel
was, in reality, some months older, and
where would she see a handsomer or more
charming young man ?

'No,' she said to Elsie, who was advocat-
ing the advantages of foreign travel, 'I will
not let him go so far away, I know something would happen to him, and it would
be most foolish and wrong of me to do it ;
for I believe'—she lowered her voice—'we
are an unfortunate family. Last spring,' she
went on after a pause, 'I wanted Frederick
to sell Alkerton and go back to Devonshire,
but, would you believe it ? he would not do
it ; he is very obstinate sometimes. He said
he could only do so at a dead loss, and he
could not afford that. But I made him do
up the church.'

'But why?' said Elsie; 'I saw the church was restored. Did Mr. Fitzgerald do all that at his own expense?'

'Yes,' said Lady Eleanor, 'he did, for I made him. Frederick did not want to do it, and really I can't blame him: most expensive it was. But I am perfectly convinced that it is not safe to live on Church lands the way we have been doing, and to give nothing back. You see what has happened already; and after such a terrible warning, it is surely my duty to be a little extra careful of Lionel. Look what happened to the Pophams, who lived here before us: I heard the whole story the first time I went over to Bulcote. I forget exactly what it was, but I know they broke their necks or something, and it was the eldest son it happened to.'

Lady Eleanor was apt to be a little inco herent in her vehemence, and Elsie looked at her rather puzzled.

'And did the Freemans warn you then?' she asked. 'Did they advise you to restore the church?'

'No, it was my own idea,' answered Lady Eleanor with a little pride. 'Frederick says it is nonsense and waste of money, but we shall see. When a thing is *right*, what does a little expense signify?'

It seemed almost as if Alkerton were to become Elsie's permanent home, for Lady Eleanor declared herself quite unable to live without her young companion; but an urgent letter from Mrs. Lindsay recalled her to Chippingham the following spring to see her uncle, the General, who was alarmingly ill. The poor old gentleman had felt his nephew's death acutely, and it had told upon him a good deal. All that autumn he had been visibly feebler, though he made no complaint; and the cold winter, followed by a colder spring, had weakened him still further. He was now seized with an attack of bronchitis, and for some days his life was in danger; though when Elsie came home he was beginning to mend, and his recovery was steady though slow. During Elsie's absence Mrs. Lindsay had been chiefly occupied with Ernest Maynard; but when he had ceased talking about his wife and infant daughter, and the novelty of his bereavement had worn off, she began to feel dull, and longed for her niece to come home. Now the General's health engrossed Mrs. Lindsay's thoughts entirely.

Elsie did not like to go away again, as her presence pleased her uncle in his still weak state; but as the spring wore on she began to turn her thoughts to Rossie, and her father wrote expressing a wish to see her in the summer. No sooner, however, had the General recovered from his bronchitis than he began to take his old attacks again; with this difference, that he made sure each time that he was going to die, and insisted upon sending for any of his relations who might be within reach to witness his last moments. This had happened twice, and· Elsie, thinking there was nothing really to be alarmed about, prepared to start for Scotland in June; the General appearing to resign himself to the plan. Two days before her proposed journey, however, he suddenly seemed to take in that she was really going to leave him, and inquired how long she would be away. Elsie said about a month or six weeks. The General fidgeted, and said by and by, 'Can ye get a telegraph at Rossie?'

'There is a telegraph office at Drumsheugh, Uncle Henry,' replied Elsie rather reluctantly.

'Drumsheugh! That's ten miles off. I don't think,' he said looking at his wife, 'she'll get back in time to see me die.'

Mrs. Lindsay gesticulated imperatively from her corner unseen by her husband, and Elsie said in a cheerful tone: 'Are you not feeling so well, Uncle Henry? I will put off going for a little till you are stronger.'

'Yes, yes, my dear, put off for a little,' said the old man fretfully. 'I'll not trouble you long.'

Elsie wrote home accordingly to put off her visit, upon which the General rallied immediately, and became more like his old self than he had been for a year; but as he showed symptoms of a relapse whenever his niece's departure was hinted at, she at length gave up hopes of going to Scotland that summer. She might have gone in autumn as far as the General's health was concerned; but when she proposed to do so, her father wrote to the effect that, as she had let all the good weather go by, she might just wait for another year. He did not wish her to come and catch her death of cold, especially as he understood from Mrs. Lindsay that she had a cough.

Elsie was really not feeling strong; and when, that same autumn, her friend Rosamond Seathwaite wrote to say that she was going to take Mona to the south of France for the winter, and was most anxious that Elsie should accompany them, even Mrs. Lindsay urged her niece to accept the invitation. Whether from weakness of body or sadness of mind, Elsie felt indifferent, and disinclined to move from where she was unless it was her positive duty to do so;

but she could not resist her friend's loving
entreaties, and went; and once in the sunny
Riviera much of her old vigour came back
to her. Rosamond's companionship, too, was
a great delight, and did her much good; and
Mona, now grown a very sweet, though quiet
little maiden, became especially devoted to
Hans, whom Elsie could not find it in her
heart to leave behind her. Poor little gentle
Hans, whose eyes had become so pathetic
now that his mistress fancied that her long
and frequent absences were making him old
before his time, and bringing premature white
hairs round his little brown nose.

CHAPTER IX.

'Er ist gereist, kommt aus Paris und Rheims
Und bringt sein treu altenglisch Herz zurück.'

THE little party of friends having spent the winter very pleasantly at San Remo, were on their way back to England in May, and only stopped to spend a week or ten days in Paris.

Rosamond was, upon the whole, well in health, and had long since recovered from the shock to her nerves, but her spirits were still variable, which a little disappointed Elsie. She was very much as she had been at Alkerton before her husband's death, except that, alone with Elsie and Mona, there was nothing to provoke and irritate her, and her temper was consequently sweeter. The troublesome law business, consequent on Sir Roger's eccentric will, was ended, and the will set aside on the ground of insanity.

Elsie, knowing Rosamond's former history, longed to speak to her about Ponsonby, and was often on the point of doing so, but there was a reserve about her friend which kept her back, and she did not dare even to mention his name in a casual way, as she knew that Rose was quite sharp enough to perceive that she had done it with a purpose, and might, indeed probably would, be displeased.

Whilst Elsie was at Alkerton the winter before, she had received a letter from Ponsonby, who, it appeared, had gone to Chippingham in hopes of seeing her, and was disappointed at not finding her there. He had gone to the Elms, he said, in order to make his adieux to her and to Mrs. Lindsay, before undertaking a voyage round the world, as he would probably be absent for a few years. Elsie was grieved and perplexed by this letter: she thought if she had seen

Ponsonby she might have understood something of his motives and purposes. She could not help speaking of it to Lady Eleanor, and expressing her regret, to which the latter replied in her off-hand way that she supposed the poor man thought he had no chance with Rose, as there was a report that she was going to marry Sir George Seathwaite; although, Lady Eleanor added, she did not for her part think such an event likely to happen, as probably Rose had had more than enough of the family. Elsie's intercourse with Rosamond showed her that there was no truth whatever in this report, but she was sure her friend was not happy.

But on the last day of their stay in Paris a most unexpected incident occurred. Elsie was strolling along the Rue de Rivoli alone, Rosamond and Mona having gone to lunch with an acquaintance, when the sound of unmistakable English voices caught her ear; and the street was presently obstructed by an English family, consisting of nine children,

who were marching along in threes, their
parents bringing up the rear.

Paterfamilias stopped Elsie and demanded :
' Ou est le omnibus pour—pour——'

' Aller,' suggested his wife.

' Pour aller a Napoleon's tombe ?'

' Monsieur,' began Elsie, fearing he might
be offended if she spoke English, ' Je ne sais
pas—I don't know when the omnibuses run ;'
and at the same moment the lady exclaimed,
' Why, John, it is Miss Ross !'

Mr. Freeman, for he it was, shook hands
with Elsie heartily, saying, ' I ask your
pardon, I am sure, for taking you for a
Frenchwoman. I wish I was at home again
with all my heart, but now we *are* here, I
suppose we must see the sights.'

' I am afraid I can't help you,' said Elsie.

' Well, here's a native, I'll ask him,' and
Mr. Freeman made a rush across the pave-
ment, and pouncing upon a young man who
was passing, loudly demanded ' Napoleon's
tombe ?'

The stranger gazed upon him for a minute

without speaking, and then quietly gave him
the desired information in English. It was
not till the Freeman family had passed on
that Elsie recognised Ponsonby, who had
stood waiting until she had done speaking
to them, and now greeted her, smiling at
her astonishment.

'And who, Miss Ross, are your charming
friends?' he inquired, as by one consent they
turned and crossed over into the Tuileries
Gardens.

'They are neighbours at Alkerton. I
never dreamt of meeting them in Paris, nor
you either, Mr. Ponsonby.'

'It is very extraordinary our meeting,'
replied Ponsonby gravely, 'at least it would
have been if I had not happened to know you
were here; but I saw Mrs. Lindsay lately,
and she told me where you were—and *whom
you were with.*'

Elsie looked up quickly at the last words.

'I wondered to meet you here, Miss Ross,'
went on Ponsonby, breaking a twig off a
shrub, and crushing it in his hand as he

spoke, 'seeing that Mrs. Lindsay did not deem your associates desirable for you.'

'No, but she deemed that—that I had better go abroad,' said Elsie with an embarrassed laugh. 'Are you going to stay some time in Paris, Mr. Ponsonby?'

'That will depend,' replied Ponsonby with great suavity, 'upon whether I succeed in what I came for.'

He walked on thoughtfully for a few paces, and then suddenly assuming an air of gaiety, said to his companion—

'And what are your first impressions of Paris, Miss Ross? and have you bought a great many dresses? Is it not a very delightful city? This avenue of trees, with the Arc de Triomphe at the end and all those nice figures on the top of it, you know, is one of the things I admire most. Do you think I may come and see Lady Seathwaite?'

'Yes,' said Elsie, 'come.' She said it bluntly, feeling utterly unable to reply in her companion's strain. 'And come to-night, for we are going away to-morrow.'

Ponsonby became grave again instantly. 'At what hour,' said he, 'may I hope to find Lady Seathwaite disengaged?'

They were now opposite the hotel, and Elsie prepared to go in. 'I will tell her you are coming at five o'clock this afternoon,' she said. 'And I—I *hope* she will be in.' She gave him her hand as if to wish him good luck, and went in quickly.

Rosamond received Elsie's intimation that Mr. Ponsonby was coming to call upon her at five o'clock with an affectation of extreme indifference, merely remarking that she supposed they would want some more cake for tea. This gave Elsie the excuse she had been seeking for to take herself and Mona out of the way; and they set out rather late to buy the cake, which Elsie contrived should be a very lengthy business. When at last they could delay no longer, and came in, Ponsonby was still sitting with Rose; and both had a look of content upon their faces which was not difficult to read. Rosamond was apparently glad to see her and

Mona, however, and scolded them for the length of time they had stayed out.

'A whole hour to buy one cake!' she said. 'Look at it!' And she uncovered it and held it up to derision.

'But Elsie would not go to any of the near shops,' piped out Mona in her childish voice, 'because Mr. Ponsonby does not like their kinds of cakes.'

Elsie felt it hard that she should be so mocked at for her well-meant little plot, which after all had answered very well; but Rosamond continued in a mocking humour, and it was not until long after Mona had gone to bed that she would bestow any confidence upon Elsie.

'You are a regular little whited sepulchre,' she said that night; 'I did not know you had it in you to be so deep. So you knew all about me from the beginning. Why did you not tell me?'

'Well, Rose, if I did wrong you must forgive me. I could not at first—I knew before I ever saw you, because David had told me ; and then of course you were married. And afterwards—I might have told you at San Remo certainly, and once or twice I nearly did, but—there was something about you which made me think you would not like it. But I am *very* glad, dear Rose.'

'Are you?' said Rose. 'Well, I don't know whether it is a thing to be glad about or not. He took me by surprise, you know, as if it was a matter of course that I would jump at it, but I don't see that at all. Men are all alike,' she went on, pouting a little. 'So exceedingly cautious. He took very good care not to come near me until he was quite sure of me.'

'Until the law business about the will was settled?' said Elsie. 'But I think that was so very nice of him. He would have put you into the position of having to choose between him and Mona, and he would rather have the pain of waiting.'

'It is a pain he did not seem to feel very much,' said Rose. 'The thing was settled long ago, and where was he, if you please ?

Amusing himself with Queen Emma in the Sandwich Islands. Besides,' she added, with her face turned away, 'suppose it had been given against me?'

But Elsie declined to argue upon this possibility.

'It was not—it would not have been,' she said. But she knew from that moment that her friend would have consented to give up her child, and live apart from her, rather than from the man she loved.

CHAPTER X.

'Let me not to the marriage of true minds
Admit impediments.'

PONSONBY accompanied the party of travellers when they returned to England, and Elsie went straight back to Chippingham, as her plan was to remain there until the end of July, which was the time fixed for Rosamond's marriage, and after that event go on to Scotland.

She was not received with any particular enthusiasm by her aunt or Miss Maynard; indeed, she found herself rather *de trop*, as it was evident that something peculiarly exciting had been going on, into the mysteries of which she was not permitted to penetrate. At first Elsie thought it must relate to Emma Dale, who had been married during

her absence abroad, and who had just started
for Canada with her husband, the outfit
having been provided by Mrs. Lindsay;
but Emma and her backwoodsman were as
nothing to Mrs. Lindsay, compared with the
present theme of her thoughts.

Sophy, it appeared, had been paying a
long visit at the Elms, and was to return in
summer. Her name was not often mentioned, but when it did occur, she was
spoken of with pomp as 'dear Sophia,' or
'our late beloved inmate;' and Elsie, hap-
pening to say regretfully that she was sorry
she had missed seeing 'dear old Sophy,' was
most severely reproved, and was quite in
disgrace for the rest of the day.

'If you permit yourself to speak thus of
Sophia,' said Mrs. Lindsay, 'who is equal to
yourself in social standing, and superior in
many points infinitely more important, I
do not know whither, Elspeth, a longer
course of association with the worldly and
unscrupulous may lead you.'

'Times are changed,' thought Elsie; but

she accepted the rebuke in silence, merely
taking the first opportunity of asking Miss
Maynard whether Sophy were going to be
married, and if so, to whom ?   But she
received no definite answer.

'N—no, oh no,' Miss Maynard said.   'I
have no reason to suppose so, none whatever, dear.'   And she seemed so ill at ease
that Elsie good-naturedly changed the subject and put by her curiosity for the present.

The General had now become much
feebler, and a good deal deafer, and his wife
did not, as before, go to him about all her
schemes and perplexities ; it troubled the
old man, who wished to be left in peace.
He liked having Elsie with him, and she
made him her chief care during the six
weeks she remained at Chippingham.

When the middle of July came she was
allowed to go back to Rose, who was in
London, at her parents' house in Cadogan
Place.   Elsie was glad to go, although from
any experience she had had of brides, she
expected to be entirely the giver, not the

receiver, of sympathy.   But she need not have misjudged her friend ; whatever Rosamond's faults might be, she was not a selfish woman, and she was as affectionate to Elsie, and as interested about all her affairs, as if she had none of her own to occupy her thoughts.   She made Elsie tell her all about Chippingham, 'to amuse her,' she said ; but in reality she wanted to give the girl advice about her future plans.   Elsie told her that she was going home to Rossie that year, of which Rose approved.

'Of course,' she said, 'you ought to be with your father.'

'Yes,' said Elsie ; 'and if I find he likes it, I think I will just stay on.'

Rosamond turned the matter seriously over in her mind, and took Ponsonby into her counsels.

'I am very sorry for Elsie,' she said.   'I do not know where that poor girl is to live. She is quite pleased now at the thoughts of going home, but I am certain she won't be able to stand Euphemia and the children.

Then she will go and stay with Aunt Eleanor, and be dragged into a marriage with Lionel. I've no patience with them——'

'A marriage with Lionel!' said Ponsonby. 'Never! she is a great deal too good for that boy.'

'I do not say that she would have him,' said Rose. 'I do not suppose she would. She does not even see that he is in love with her (which is very odd); but when Aunt Eleanor sets her heart upon a thing, she will get her own way sooner or later.'

'But it is absurd!' said Ponsonby; 'it must be prevented. Would you wish— would you like her to live with us?'

'I do not think she would do it, William,' said Rose with a smile, which went far to repay her lover for his really generous proposal. 'She must pay us long visits, and we must defeat Aunt Eleanor if we can. I would give her a hint about Lionel, but she is so innocent it might only do harm.'

The wedding took place in London, and was very quiet. The only guests, besides

Elsie, were Rosamond's parents, her two
brothers, her sister Blanche, and Lady
Eleanor; Lionel was not invited, and Mr.
Fitzgerald excused himself on the plea of
illness. Elsie was specially desired to bring
Hans, and did so at Mona's earnest entreaty,
though she would have preferred to leave
him behind. Rosamond insisted upon doing
everything herself; she arranged the flowers,
entertained the company, and behaved, as
Lady Mary rather querulously observed, as
if somebody else were being married.

Lady Eleanor proposed to carry off Elsie
and Mona to Alkerton as soon as the wedding
was over, there to remain until she and Mr.
Fitzgerald went to Scotland, for they were to
spend the autumn at Ardvoira.

'We will all go to Scotland together,' she
said, when she heard of Elsie's intention of
going home. 'That will be a charming
plan, Elsie, and you shall pay me a visit at
Ardvoira before you go to your father.'

Elsie demurred at this, but Lady Eleanor
would hear of no objection.

'No indeed,' she said, 'I cannot let you off, Elsie. The house at Ardvoira is an absolute den of disorder; I shall never put it right without your help. Then you will like the scenery and all that; Lionel is dying to show it to you—it is quite his hobby just now. You know he is never happy unless *you* are there,' and Lady Eleanor looked as if this last argument must infallibly settle the question, but Rosamond took her friend aside on the first opportunity.

'Don't go to Ardvoira with her,' she said. 'You will not if you are wise.'

'I do think it would be better not,' Elsie said; 'but how can I refuse Lady Eleanor? It *is* a trying journey with Mr. Fitzgerald—and then if there is nothing comfortable in the house—and she is not very strong, you know——'

'Stuff and nonsense!' interrupted Rosamond with energy. 'I really can't think, Elsie, how you can let yourself be made a slave of by that woman! She is as well able to do things for herself as you or I. There

is nothing the matter with her—except selfish-
ness. And you heard what she said about
Lionel.'

'That is her way of talking,' said Elsie.
'Lionel means nothing; but for many reasons
I would rather not go to Ardvoira.'

She dropped the subject, for she felt it
was one upon which she and Rosamond
would never agree. Rosamond had no
sympathy with Lady Eleanor, whose charms
did not appeal to her in the least; and she
had very little patience with Lionel. She
could not help rather liking that young man
when he was actually before her, and always
treated him in a pleasant, cousinly way; but
the moment he was out of her sight she
remembered his faults rather than his virtues,
and being energetic herself, she had no tolera-
tion for idleness, especially in a man. She
was ambitious, too, as well as active, and was
no sooner married than she began to stir up
her husband to distinguish himself in some
way. She would have liked him best to go
into Parliament; but finding after repeated

efforts that politics were not Ponsonby's vocation, she set him to write books of travel, and illustrate them with his own drawings, since he had failed to make a reputation as a great painter.   But all this came to pass in later years, and in the meantime the newly married pair went to finish Ponsonby's interrupted tour round the world, from which 'urgent private affairs,' in other words, the news of Sir George Seathwaite's marriage to a cousin of his own, had recalled him in the spring.

We must now return to Elsie, who went with Lady Eleanor to Alkerton, Lionel having already gone to Scotland.   Elsie had not really disregarded her friend's warning ; and her eyes being now partly opened to Lady Eleanor's schemes concerning her, she spent many anxious hours in pondering upon how she had best undeceive her.   For Elsie to become Lionel's wife was an impossibility, an incongruity not to be dreamt of for a moment. She did not seriously believe the boy to be in love with her, but it was undoubtedly better that they should meet as little as possible until this foolish fancy had passed away. She therefore remained firm to her intention of returning to Chippingham, until one day she received a letter from Miss Maynard which had the effect of materially altering her plans. The letter contained the solution of the enigma which had puzzled her at Chippingham, but which she had since forgotten.

'THE ELMS, CHIPPINGHAM,
'*August* 15*th*.

'MY DEAREST ELSIE—During the press of engagements which has rendered your dear aunt (busy as she always is) more than usually occupied, she has named me as her substitute to convey to you tidings which, we trust, will give you *heartfelt pleasure*, while they cannot fail to *surprise* you. I have so much to tell you, dear Elsie, that I feel quite embarrassed how to begin— *embarras de richesses!* Do you remember, dear, asking me a curiously *àpropos* question regarding dear Sophia? I was able to

answer truthfully at that time that she was
not engaged to be married ; but, my love,
she now is so and will (D.V.) shortly become
the bride of my dear nephew Ernest!   This
will take you by surprise, as it did me ; but
to your dear aunt's *keen vision* the progress
of the attachment has long been apparent.
She observed dear Sophia's unusual depression during her first visit to us whilst you
were abroad, and at once drew from her its
true cause ; but as Ernest had not spoken
she did not feel justified in taking any steps
in the matter.   When Sophy returned to us
in July Ernest's diffidence was still very great,
but, thanks to your aunt, it has now been
overcome, and the young people are on the
footing of *affianced lovers.*   I confess I de-
spaired of this ever being brought about, but
your dear aunt, with her usual decision, did
not allow the young people to endanger their
own happiness by *false pride*, and herself told
Ernest plainly that he had engaged the affec-
tions of a young and interesting girl whom
he would find *in the dining-room*.   The re-

sult, my love, you already know, and the
happiness of the young pair is *complete*.
The marriage will take place (D.V.) at
Michaelmas, and I know that Sophia in-
tends asking you to stand nearest to her at
the altar in the character of *bridesmaid*.
Next week our happy 'nest among the
Elms' will be deserted; your uncle and
aunt, with dear Sophia, intend going to
London for a fortnight. Very pleasant
apartments have been secured near Ken-
sington Gardens, where your amiable uncle
loves to walk, the heat there not being so
intense as in the street; while your aunt
and Sophy, with Parkins's assistance, will
busy themselves with purchases. I hope,
meanwhile, to remain with Ernest at the
vicarage and endeavour to put it in order
for its future inmate. Your aunt desires
me to inform you, with her love, of these
arrangements, as she thinks it a pity for
you to incur the *needless fatigue* and expense
of returning to Chippingham before your
Scottish visit is paid. Sophy, who has just

come in, desires her *very best love*, and wishes
that you were here. All unite in kindest
remembrances to Lady Eleanor and her
circle,—and I am ever, dearest Elsie, your
affectionate old friend,

'CECILIA MAYNARD.'

Elsie did not at first regard this letter as
bearing upon her own plans, and expressed
her indignation aloud.

'It is too bad—it really *is* too bad! She
can't leave that poor man alone. I shall not
go near them—I would not be Sophy's
bridesmaid for——'

My dear Elsie, what is the matter?' said
Lady Eleanor. 'I declare you are quite
excited.'

Elsie read the letter aloud, and Lady
Eleanor listened to it with great cool-
ness.

'Mr. Maynard is the clergyman, is he not?
Oh yes, very nice that he should marry her
niece. Rather an amusing letter, I think;
it is so like your Aunt Caroline to arrange

it all.   Well, Elsie, that quite settles it, you
see—you come to Scotland with me.'

Elsie bit her lips, she saw how incautious
she had been ; but there was no drawing
back now without seriously vexing her
hostess, so she yielded with as good a
grace as she could, and the Scottish journey
was arranged for the following week.

Little Mona, with her governess, was to
be sent to Wynchcombe ; and to her Elsie
entrusted Hans, to be taken care of until her
return.   She felt quite satisfied in doing this,
the child and the dog being inseparable ; and
the prospect of keeping Hans made Mona
perfectly happy.

PART III.

CHAPTER I.

'Sweet Wicklow mountains ! the sunlight shining
  On your green hills is a picture rare ;
  You crowd around me like young girls peeping,
  And puzzling me to say which is most fair.
  You seem to watch your own sweet faces
  Reflected in the smooth and silver sea ;
  My blessing on those lovely places,
  Though no one knows how dear they are to me.'

FIVE years is a long time out of a girl's life ; and to Elsie especially, who had gone through such varied experiences since she had left her home, the period which she had spent in England was like a lifetime in itself. She had never forgotten her home, and still looked back to it often and lovingly ; yet she had had a strong presentiment on leaving Rossie that that page in her life was over and done with for ever ; and even now it seemed impossible to be going back to it. She had something of the same feeling now as regarded Chippingham, which Miss Maynard's letter had helped to strengthen. Sophy, it appeared, had taken her place, and she would never be quite the same to Aunt Caroline again. This was, of course, partly her own doing. She had found David's relations more congenial; and yet the feeling that the Chippingham life too had slipped away from her gave her keen pain. Many a time she had felt that she must get away from Aunt Caroline in order to breathe freely, that she could not stand another day in her society; yet Elsie could not but be touched by the wonderful kindness and affection with which her aunt had always treated her; and it was to her now that her thoughts turned regretfully, far more than to her friend Miss Maynard—more even than to the kind old General.

Elsie had leisure and quiet for all these thoughts while in the train on their north-ward journey, for Lady Eleanor would stand no nonsense from her husband when *she* was travelling with him, and the least word

of complaint from the unhappy Frederick
was speedily quenched by the suggestion
that he might get into a separate carriage if
he was going to grumble, as she, Lady
Eleanor, was not going to sit there to be
annoyed.

The journey as far as Glasgow, however,
was not a very fatiguing one. Elsie had
never considered herself a very patriotic
person, nor thought it necessary to assert
the superiority of Scotland over England in
any way ; yet her soul within her was not so
dead as to deserve the curses of the Last
Minstrel ; for as she stood on the platform
of the crowded Glasgow station, watching a
miscellaneous heap of luggage being tumbled
out of the van, a smile of pleasure lit up her
face at the porter's ' Bide there a wee, till
I get a hurrly.' She had never been at
Glasgow before, and had no particular
sentiment connected with that city, yet even
the Glasgow accent, hideous as it is, sounded
friendly to her ears.

The night was spent at St. Enoch's Hotel,

and the journey next day was accomplished
partly by rail and partly by steamer. It was
between three and four in the afternoon that
the steamer was brought to a stop, to permit
the party to get into the little boat which
now drew up alongside of her.

For the last hour and a half they had
been passing through lovely scenery, and
Elsie sat on the steamer's deck watching
the gulls following in their wake, or looking
out at the green Argyllshire hills and the
soft and misty islands with a growing pain
at her heart. 'How shall I bear it?' she
said to herself, with her hands clasped tight
together; 'why did I let them bring me?'

The sudden stop of the steamer, and the
hissing noise the boiler made, startled her
out of her sad thoughts. Down below was
a little boat, which seemed perilously heaving
up and down on the waves caused by the
great steamer's paddle-wheel, for the sea
itself was as smooth as glass; and in the
boat stood a young man in gray shooting
clothes and a little gray cap. He was

steadying the ladder by which the passen-
gers were to descend, and looking up eagerly
into the steamer, his handsome, still boyish
face all alight with joyful expectation.

'Lionel! my dear boy, do be careful.
What a place to get down!'

'Steady, mother! give me your other
hand—you are all right. Now, Elsie!' and
before Elsie could think, she was fairly lifted
down in Lionel's strong arms and placed beside his mother in the stern, while he looked
at her with an evident delight which called
forth an answering smile in spite of herself.

'Take care, Frederick!' in an agonised
voice from Lady Eleanor, as the terrified
Frederick seemed about to precipitate himself into the sea, and Lionel, clutching his
stepfather's leg, pulled him into the boat.

'I wish you would not get in like that,'
she said, as her husband sank down, panting,
amongst the luggage; 'it does make me so
nervous. You must stay there now, I
suppose, or you will upset the boat, and we
shall all be drowned.'

Another boat now came up to take off
the servants and the heavier luggage, and
the big steamer went on her way. Lionel,
taking one pair of oars, seated himself
opposite, and talked to his mother, answering her questions and complaints in a cheery
pleasant way, while his eyes strayed to
Elsie's face. She herself sat looking out,
wistful and abstracted. As yet they could
gain no view of the house, which was hidden
by a point they had to round before reaching
the little harbour. The sun of early autumn
shone softly through a veil of mist; the sea
was silvery gray in the distance where the
shadows of the clouds left lines of light; the
far-off islands were faint and yet distinct,
their outlines nearly white against the pale
gold sky. Near them now, the rocky point
stood out bold and rugged, and by the boat's
sides every stone and shell and bit of sea-
weed could be seen as plainly through the
depths of clear green water as in the
shallowest stream.

The point was passed, and they entered

a small loch or narrow inlet, and drew near
to the little pier.   The house was just visible
among the trees, a long low house, blue-
slated, with white walls, rough cast, or
harled as it is called in Scotland.   Behind
the house was a bank of natural wood—oak,
birch, mountain-ash, and hazel—still clothed
in the deep green of late summer.   The
thin line of smoke, which rose up in the still
air straight from the chimneys, showed blue
against the dark background.   The house
was fenced round by hills ; sharp rocky hills,
steep green hills, heathery hills, stretching
away indefinitely, and vaguely termed 'the
shootings.'   A wooded gorge ran up into
this wild region, and lost itself in its
windings ; through it a brown river ran,
murmuring amongst the trees, foaming between narrow walls of rock past the house,
till near the landing-place it took its final
leap, and dashed into the still gray sea.

The landing was effected without difficulty,
and the party walked to the house, Lionel
keeping close to Elsie's side, but speaking

little, for which she was grateful.   The house
was surrounded by smooth green turf; and
large myrtle and fuchsia bushes, untouched
by frost in that mild, damp climate, grew
before the door.   The rooms were low, and
rather small, but looked homelike to Elsie's
eyes, though Lady Eleanor groaned over
them as 'uninhabitable.'   The library, where
tea awaited them, was rather like the cabin
of a ship; floor, walls, and ceiling being all
of varnished pine; books were there in
plenty, but invisible behind their panelled
doors.

'How musty the house does smell,' said
Lady Eleanor, sinking into a chair behind
the tea-table.   'All houses in the Highlands
have that smell, I think.   It is very odd; I
hope it is not rats, Elsie?'

'Oh no!' said Elsie faintly, 'rats smell
quite different; I *like* this smell.   Shall I
make tea for you, dear Lady Eleanor? you
look tired.'

'Do,' said Lady Eleanor, 'it would be a
charity.'   She rose out of the rather hard

arm-chair, and stretched herself discontentedly on the still harder sofa. 'Of all detestable countries to travel in, I do think Scotland is the most detestable,' she said. ' No, Frederick, you need not argue——' as Mr. Fitzgerald uttered an inarticulate grunt. 'What I have gone through on this journey no words can tell.'

Lionel looked a little vexed, but did not contradict his mother. Elsie thought him graver and more manly than he used to be; he was attentive to every one's comfort, and particularly gentle and thoughtful towards herself, seeming to know instinctively what she was feeling, and avoiding everything which might distress her. He kept near her and watched her, but spoke little; and her first evening in David's home passed more peacefully than she had dared to hope.

CHAPTER II.

' I now can see with better eyes ;
And worldly grandeur I despise,
And fortune with her gifts and lies.'

HAD a traveller been going along the road
which passed the gate of Ardvoira, he would
have come in time to the head of the loch,
some three miles farther on. Here stood
the parish church ; a small, square, white
building, harled and blue - slated like the
houses, and adorned with a little belfry.
There was a village, or what was dignified
by the name of one ; a few miserable-looking,
thatched cottages, from whose chimneyless
roofs the peat smoke curled, giving forth a
strange, pungent fragrance. The manse was
close by, shut in by shrubs, which from
neglect had grown into a thick, tangled
wilderness, overgrown by brambles. It had

an uninhabited look, but a minister existed
nevertheless; an aged man, whose wife had
died some twenty years before; his sons had
grown up and gone to distant towns; and
he, with no servant but an old Highland
housekeeper, lived in a corner of the
neglected manse.   He was almost too old
to carry on his duties, and an assistant and
successor was in course of being appointed,
which occasioned considerable excitement
throughout the parish.

About a mile farther up the glen was
another dwelling, nestling among the hills,
which was a remarkable contrast to the dirty,
deserted-looking manse.   This was Glen
Torran, the residence of Mr. Carmichael, a
retired East India merchant, who in his early
years had led a seafaring life, but now devoted himself to farming.   By birth Mr. Carmichael was a Lowlander, but an innate love
of sport and a certain fancy for the Highlands had led him to buy Glen Torran, where
he and his wife had now spent many happy
years.   Their children were all grown up and

settled in life ; their eldest daughter Isabella
had married Lord Ochil, who, it may be
remembered, was Captain Ross's neighbour
at Drumsheugh. Mrs. Carmichael's motherly
heart could not be satisfied without children
about her, and she generally contrived to
have with her some of her numerous grandchildren, who naturally looked upon Glen
Torran as an earthly paradise. A very bright
little place it looked on this August morning,
with its gay flower-beds, trim hedges, and
little porch clustered over with creepers.
Mrs. Carmichael was weeding in the garden,
a pleasant sight in her shady straw bonnet,
and gown thriftily tucked up. She was a
charming old lady, stout, fair, and comely ;
perhaps sixty-five years of age, but her figure
was still upright, and her complexion as fresh
as that of many a girl of twenty.

Her two little grandsons, Walter and
Hughie Forbes, Lady Ochil's youngest
children, were sharing with the wasps the
last remaining gooseberries.

'Somebody is calling you, grandmamma,'

said one of the children, and Mrs. Carmichael heard her name shouted from the house door. 'Catharine! Catharine!' called her husband impatiently.

'What is it you want?' she said, digging viciously at a dandelion root with her trowel.

Mr. Carmichael came forward—a hale old gentleman, with gray whiskers and a wide-awake hat.

'Here's Mr. M'Phail,' said he.

Mrs. Carmichael gathered herself up and came forward, all smiles, to greet the aged minister.

'How do you do, Mr. M'Phail?' she called into his deaf ears. 'It's a far walk for you. Walter, speak to me.' She drew the little boy close to her and whispered, 'Go and get your faces washed for luncheon, both of you, and tell Christina to lay a place for Mr. M'Phail. Say "How do you do" first. Now run away, that's a man. Come away in, Mr. M'Phail.'

'Catharine,' said Mr. Carmichael, 'the

minister says the Fitzgeralds are come.
You'll need to go and see them.'

'Indeed? Have you seen the Ardvoira
people, Mr. M'Phail?'

'I will haf seen the young Laird,' answered
the old minister,—'and he iss a fine yowth.'

'Yes, yes, a very nice lad,' said Mrs. Carmichael, 'but have his family arrived?'

This question caused the old man some
perplexity, but on its being repeated in various keys by both his host and hostess,
they at last learnt that 'young Ardvoira's
father and his mother, and aal his family, and
his men-servants and his women-servants and
his kists,' had undoubtedly been seen to dis-
embark at Ardvoira pier the preceding evening.

'You'll need to go and see them this afternoon, Catharine,' repeated Mr. Carmichael.

'Tuts!' said his wife, putting another wing
of chicken on the minister's plate—'I'm not
going to call upon people before they're unpacked.'

Her husband, however, nothing daunted,

continued to offer the same suggestion at intervals all through luncheon, concluding with the remark, 'Very uncivil not to go and see them when you know they're there.'

'Well, go and call yourself,' retorted his wife, 'and I am sure they'll wish you at the back of beyont.'

As Mr. Carmichael had never been known to call upon any one in his life, except upon the most urgent business, this repartee was rather a symptom of yielding on his wife's part.

The minister, after fortifying himself with a pinch of snuff, now observed that he had had a 'fery handsome dinner,' and intimated further that 'this feesit was the commaince-ment of his yearly diet of feesitation.' His hostess, understanding this speech to be in-dicative of a desire to offer up a prayer in the kitchen, at once conducted the aged pastor thither, and summoned the household. This done, she returned to her husband, observing—

'That poor old man gets dirtier every day

—he's a perfect disgrace to be seen. What's that woman of his thinking of that she doesn't take and wash him ?'

Mr. Carmichael agreed in lamenting with her the minister's somewhat unsavoury condition, adding, that it was a poor return for the expense to which the heritors had lately been put in supplying the manse with water.

' Poor old body ! I'll tell you what, James,' said Mrs. Carmichael, after a short pause for reflection, ' I *will* call at Ardvoira to-day if you'll order the carriage. And I'll take him with me, and drop him at the manse; he's not fit for those long travels on his feet.'

Accordingly Mrs. Carmichael, having changed her everyday dress, and put on her best bonnet and cloak, set forth, accompanied by the minister, and by little Hughie, who was also, his grandmother said, ' better off his feet.'

There had been rain during the night, and a touch of sharpness in the air gave the first signs of the approach of autumn. The sun shone brightly, and the loch was blue, flecked

over with little white waves; the opposite
hills were distinct and clear. The breeze
swept over the hills, bringing out all their
wild sweet scents; the flowers were at their
best and gayest, heather and bluebells and
golden-rod, and the patches of deep green
bracken were beginning to turn a golden-
brown. Lower down, the sweet bog-myrtle
grew thickly, mixed with starry white grass
of Parnassus and the orange seeds of the bog
asphodel.

'Jump out and ring the bell, Hughie,'
said Mrs. Carmichael when they reached
Ardvoira, 'and see that you behave yourself,
now, and speak when you are spoken to.'

Thus admonished, her grandson, climbing
upon the scraper and seizing the bell with
both hands, rang a peal which quickly brought
the astonished man-servant to the door. In
answer to Mrs. Carmichael's question, he
replied that he did not know whether her
ladyship was at home, but would inquire.
In a few minutes, however, she was admitted,
and welcomed with great cordiality by Lady

Eleanor, who well remembered her kind old friend, and longed for somebody to whom she might pour out her grievances.

'So good of you to come, dear Mrs. Carmichael,' said she. 'You find us in a shocking state of disrepair. The journey in itself was enough to knock one up, and then the worries I have gone through with servants and luggage, and Frederick being ill and no doctor!'

'I am sorry to hear Mr. Fitzgerald is ill.'

'Oh, he is never well, and he is such a bad traveller. He will get over it; but, my dear Mrs. Carmichael, just fancy this! The cook who came with us yesterday has been in bed ever since—says the air of the Highlands does not suit her—and the consequence is, we must do all the work ourselves, I suppose. It is fortunate I brought Elsie—oh, by the way, you know Elsie Ross? such a nice girl——'

'I knew her as a child,' interrupted Mrs. Carmichael, 'my daughter Isabella was very fond of her. I heard she was coming with you.'

'Well, you shall see her by and by, but about the cook, what do you advise? I don't like to send her straight back, poor thing, she was so highly recommended, and she does make excellent clear soup.'

An inquiry into the cook's symptoms now took place, and from this the talk diverged to diseases in general, and thence to all the deaths which had taken place in the two ladies' acquaintance since they last met.

Mrs. Carmichael's kindly sympathy led her friend on to talk of David, who had been a frequent guest at Glen Torran in former days.

'It is very trying for me to come here, very!' said Lady Eleanor, drying her eyes; 'it is for Lionel's sake I do it. I could not have faced it without Elsie, but to make those two dear children happy is all I live for now.'

Mrs. Carmichael looked at her in some astonishment. 'Is Lionel?—I always understood——' She hesitated.

'Yes, Elsie was engaged to my poor David,' replied Lady Eleanor. '*I* never

thought them suited, and I don't believe the
child knew her own mind, but I am the last
person to throw obstacles in the way of any
one's happiness. Many mothers, I daresay,
would have different views for their sons, but
Lionel is all I have now, and if his heart is
set on this—— For my part, I don't approve
of worldly, ambitious marriages. I don't think
they are right.'

She shook her head in a chastened manner, and rose from her seat. 'Now I should
really like to show you the house,' she said,
'and see what you think can be done about
the game larder; it is *so* inconvenient, and
I expect a party next month.' She led the
way downstairs. Little Hughie, in obedience
to a sign from his grandmother, had long
since left the room, and the sound of his
voice, which seemed to issue from a dark
passage, made her pause on her way to the
larder.

'Ah!' said Lady Eleanor, 'your little
grandson has found his way to the storeroom. He is quite safe, Elsie will take

charge of him.   You would like to speak to
Elsie—will you come in here ?'

It was a large, light storeroom into which
Lady Eleanor conducted her visitor.   Elsie,
with her sleeves tucked up, and a holland
apron tied round her, was kneeling on the
floor, surrounded by numerous brown paper
packages, which Katie, a stout-armed Highland lass, was putting away under her directions.

Hughie, perched upon a flour-barrel, with
his little legs crossed, was complacently
munching an apple, while he gave his opinion
from time to time on the quality of the goods
which were being unpacked, or addressed
searching questions to Katie respecting the
young man he had seen her walking with on
Sunday.

'My dear, I will not disturb you,' said
Mrs. Carmichael, after Elsie had been introduced to her; 'you seem to be in your
work.   I remember you so well at Drumsheugh when you were a little girl.'   She held
Elsie's hand, and patted it kindly.   'Don't

let that little smout be a trouble to you,' she said smiling at Hughie as she went away.

'Yes, a remarkably pretty girl,' she said when she was alone with Lady Eleanor; 'but—my dear, excuse me — don't let her wear herself to death.   She doesn't look to me strong.'

'No,' said Lady Eleanor, not in the least offended, 'I don't think she is—none of us are strong; and of course all this is a great fatigue.   I should not be surprised if she were laid up—not the least; and I am the worst person in the world to look after any one who is delicate.'

'Oh no! the Highland air is a fine thing; and it does a girl no harm to have something to do; but that child wants feeding up.'

'Indeed she does,' said Lady Eleanor, 'the misfortune is that we have no cook; but Elsie is always slight, and her figure is round if you come to look at it.   I was much thinner as a girl; indeed, before I married, the doctors thought I was going into a decline.'

There was no more to be said; but when Elsie and Hughie, after a course of washing and brushing, presented themselves in the drawing-room, Mrs. Carmichael spoke affectionately to the girl, pressed her to come often to Glen Torran, and when she left, insisted on taking her in the carriage as far as the shore, that the salt breezes might blow some colour into her pale cheeks.

CHAPTER III.

'Die Welt treibt fort ihr Wesen,
   Die Leute kommen und gehn,
Als wärst du nie gewesen,
   Als wäre nichts geschehn,
Wie sehn' ich mich aufs neue
   Hinaus in Wald und Flur !
Ob ich mich gräm', mich freue,
   Du bleibst mir treu, Natur.'

THE domestic difficulties at Ardvoira were gradually smoothed over. The cook recovered, so did Mr. Fitzgerald. Nearly a fortnight had passed since their arrival, and Elsie had grown accustomed to her surroundings. She had grown to love the place for its own sake as well as for David's, and its beauty gave her intense, though melancholy pleasure. She could scarcely bear the thought of leaving it, even to go home, though she felt that it was time her visit came to an end. Lionel contrived to

be constantly with her : whether she climbed
the hill, or wandered on the shore, or went
into the garden or up the glen, he was sure
to appear, and linger with her till the last
possible moment.   He never said a word
which could give her pain, and was always
most thoughtful and gentle with her, but
she could not help feeling that for his sake,
if for no other reason, it would be better
she should go.   She therefore told Lady
Eleanor that she must go to Rossie the
following week, adhering to her resolution
in spite of all opposition.

'Really, Elsie, it is very hard upon me,'
said Lady Eleanor.   'If you go, I shall
have to entertain all those dreadful creatures
by myself.   And you were beginning to
look so well! why, at first people thought
I overworked you, and they may think so
still if you don't get more colour.   I should
not wonder, now, if they did.   I think it
very likely.'

'Nobody could possibly think so,' replied
Elsie ; 'but, indeed, Lady Eleanor, I must

go.   Think! I have not seen my father for
five years and a half.'

'Well, of course if you put it in that
way; but *I* believe, Elsie, it is nothing but
obstinacy; and, say what you will, obstinacy
is a very bad feature in any character.'

She continued to lament over the arrival
of her guests, and the fatigues which she
would have to undergo on their account,
till Elsie began to think herself the most
selfish of mortals.

'You will have Blanche,' she suggested
faintly, 'and Constance.'

'Blanche!' said Lady Eleanor with
withering scorn.   'Now, I ask you, Elsie,
of what use is Blanche likely to be?'

'I like Blanche,' said Elsie.   'We have
become great friends now.'

'Friends!   I daresay—but as to her
being the smallest use to me——! That
girl,' she continued in a tragic tone, 'does
nothing—absolutely nothing, except please
herself.   She will lecture about Buddhism
or any of her ridiculous views by the hour

together—of course every one is very much
bored. *She* does not care, and she will not
even talk to any one she does not fancy.
You may call that *haut ton* if you like; I
think it positively wrong. And as for
Constance——' she paused expressively.

'I have not seen Constance since she
was married,' said Elsie.

'Then you have missed seeing a most
degrading spectacle.'

'What!' said Elsie, opening her eyes.

'Call it what you please,' said Lady
Eleanor, leaning back and fanning herself.
'A woman who spoils her husband to that
extent, is to me absolutely revolting. You
have seen Douglas Ferrars—is he a man
before whom anybody could fall down flat?
Commonplace to the last degree! And you
remember Constance—a girl you would not
have expected to give up her own way
very readily? I never admired her much
myself, but she had a good deal of style
undoubtedly, and now she has utterly lost
any looks she ever had. Grovelling at

the feet of that man! I have no patience with her.'

'Do tell me about it, Lady Eleanor,' said Elsie, much interested. 'Does he order her about, or what?'

'Oh, I can't describe it to you,' said Lady Eleanor, rising off her chair. 'It is indescribable!'

The subject apparently ruffled her; she left the room, closing the door with a slight bang.

This conversation took place in the evening, and the post next day brought Elsie a letter from her father which caused her much disquiet. Little Patrick (or Peter as he was generally called), the elder of the twins, had taken scarlet fever. It was a mild case, but as Elsie had never had the fever, her father entirely declined receiving her at Rossie; she must 'put off her time somewhere' until all danger of infection was past.

'Oh, well then, Elsie,' said Lady Eleanor, when this letter was read to her, 'you will

stay on here and help me with my company.
How fortunate the child took it when he did,
and not later.   Do not look so anxious, my
dear; children always take these complaints,
and get over them all right.'

'It is not that,' said Elsie, 'but poor
Euphemia!   I think I ought to go and help
her to nurse him—I never take infection.'

'Now you are quite silly, Elsie, and I
am sure Mrs. Carmichael, who is a sensible
woman, will say the same' (they were going
to luncheon at Glen Torran).   'Frederick!
here is Elsie wishing to go and catch scarlet
fever.'

'Indeed!' said Mr. Fitzgerald, who had
a great dread of infection, looking round
in alarm.   'Scarlet fever!   where?   how?
what?'

'Oh, not here,' said his wife, 'and I don't
mean to let her go.   Come, Elsie, and get
ready for Glen Torran.'

Mrs. Carmichael likewise treated with
disdain the idea of Elsie's going to nurse
her little brother.

'It would be a tempting of Providence,' said that lady. 'And when her father, honest man, does not even want her! Make your mind easy, Elsie, my dear, and come and visit me when you are wearied of Ardvoira.'

'But I can't spare her, Mrs. Carmichael,' said Lady Eleanor. 'Do try and look a little cheerful, Elsie, it is very good for you not to have your own way in everything. You were really beginning to get too independent.'

'Indeed, Lady Eleanor,' said Elsie, 'I am only too glad—in a way—to stay, and of course I will, as you and Mrs. Carmichael are both so kind as to say so.'

Thus it was settled that Elsie must remain at Ardvoira, and she could only hope, to use her own words to herself, that Lionel would 'take no harm.' He was going to the Oban meeting before long, that was one comfort ; and when he returned he would bring friends with him, while other guests were expected from England ; so

the constant *tête-à-têtes* must come to an
end. In her secret heart too Elsie could
not help being glad of the reprieve ; so
she put all doubts out of her mind, and
exerted herself to take part in the conversation.

'And so you are to have a houseful,
Lady Eleanor,' said Mr. Carmichael, who
always thirsted for information about his
neighbours' doings. 'I hear you are to
entertain the whole country-side.'

'I am afraid I shall do nothing so praise-
worthy, Mr. Carmichael. My guests will
be chiefly my own relations from England,
and Lionel will bring my nephew Lord
Heathfield and a friend back from Oban
with him.'

'Oh! he is to be with the M'Nab party
at Oban, I hear.'

'I think—yes—some people of that
name,' said Lady Eleanor, with a little
inflexion of scorn in her voice. 'I know
nothing about them—Lionel picked them
up somewhere.'

Mr. Carmichael laughed heartily, with
a thorough enjoyment of the joke which
Lady Eleanor failed to understand. She
looked inquiringly at his wife, who said,
'Yes, he is very rude. James, do you
hear? you are very rude to Lady Eleanor.
But mercy me, my dear! don't go about
saying you know nothing about the M'Nabs.
They're the M'Nabs of Auchenbothie, to
say nothing of Meish, Neish, and Scoura.
You mustn't take *their* name in vain.'

'It's a dreadful name,' said Lady Eleanor
somewhat sullenly.

'They were a dreadful clan in old days,
I fancy,' said Mrs. Carmichael; 'and they
let nobody forget it now, if they can help it.
They are cousins of yours, I think—at any-
rate of yours, Elsie. Are not you related
to the Stewarts of Knockbrichachan?'

'Yes,' said Elsie, 'I met a lady once—a
Mrs. Macdonald-Smith, who was a Stewart
by birth, and said she was my cousin.'

'Well, those M'Nabs,' said Mrs. Carmichael impressively, 'are the only people

the Knockbrichachans can marry without lowering themselves.'

Elsie laughed. 'It is fortunate then,' said she, 'that there are such people, else the Knockbrichachans would have to remain unmarried, I suppose. But by the way, Mr. Macdonald-Smith——'

'That was her second husband, my dear! of course she married a M'Nab to begin with. Oh, and besides, the Macdonalds of Ardvoira! why, they are descended from the old Lords of the Isles that you read about in history—but they are nothing to the M'Nabs for all that.'

Mrs. Carmichael said all this with a twinkle in her eye, but Elsie saw that Lady Eleanor was a little annoyed; she disliked jokes and saw no sense in them.

A day or two later Lionel departed for Oban. He went with great reluctance; and his mother, after her visit to Glen Torran, treated him with marked coldness, in order to show him that she disapproved of his going at all, since he was to associate with the M'Nabs, whose very existence had become an offence to her, although she never mentioned the obnoxious name, or alluded to them in the most distant manner.

He was not many days away, and Elsie's little time of peace passed only too swiftly. The party was expected on the morrow, and she exerted herself to make Ardvoira look its best and brightest. She ransacked the garden for flowers, and brought in what she could; a few rain-washed carnations and sweet peas, china roses, and a store of beautiful Japanese anemones, both white and pink; and from outside she brought stag's horn moss and bog myrtle, late-flowering honeysuckle, and yellow and crimson bramble leaves; and ivy and rowan berries to deck the dinner table.

'Don't tire yourself, child,' said Lady Eleanor, 'or you will be as white as a sheet, and Lionel will think it is my fault; besides it is so unbecoming. What have you brought to wear in the morning? I am tired of looking at that brown homespun.'

Elsie laid down her flowers, and began to reckon up her dresses upon her fingers. 'There is the black cashmere that I wore on Sunday; and my gray with the corduroy skirt; and my blue serge; and my white serge; and my——'

'Oh, well, I daresay you have enough; but I never heard of the white serge before. Put it on! I want to see how you look in it.'

Elsie left her flowers reluctantly and went.

'That is lovely!' said Lady Eleanor when she reappeared. 'That gold-brown embroidery is simply perfect—isn't it, Frederick? and yet the dress is so simply made. Turn round—let Frederick see the back.'

Mr. Fitzgerald, who was a connoisseur in ladies' dresses, expressed his unqualified approval.

'Now be sure you wear it, Elsie,' said Lady Eleanor. 'Why keep your clothes boxed up until they are out of fashion?'

'It is scarcely suitable for a Highland

place,' said Elsie. 'One scrambles about, you know, and it will get so dirty.'

'Nonsense! put it on on Sunday then. You don't scramble to church, I suppose.'

Lionel, with Lord Heathfield and Mr. Hargrave, had met his cousins at Oban. They had preferred to take that route, in order to avoid the longer sea voyage, and also that they might visit Edinburgh and see something of Scottish scenery on their way.

At length word was brought that the steamer was in sight, boats were put out, and the Ardvoira party went down to the shore to meet their guests as they landed. There they came! two boatloads of them; Lionel first, looking very brown and handsome, and happy to be at home again; next Lord Heathfield, with his faultless collar and beautifully brushed hair; Constance Ferrars and her husband; and Blanche Mortimer, who accepted, though rather disdainfully, the assistance of Charles Hargrave, her *fiancé*.

The first greetings past, Blanche turned

from him, and hastily put her arm through
Elsie's. 'I am thankful to arrive,' she said;
'you have no idea what a bore they all are.
They have dragged me all the way round by
Oban—to see Scotland forsooth! as if I had
not seen it fifty times. It drives me perfectly
frantic to be turned into a common tourist to
please Douglas Ferrars.'

Blanche entertained the most cordial contempt for her brother-in-law, which she was
at no pains to conceal.

Lionel, foiled in his attempts to talk to
Elsie, now addressed himself to his mother.

'The M'Nabs were very kind and hospi-
table,' said he, 'but I am not sorry to get
back. They have got a capital yacht; and I
have asked young M'Nab and his sister to
come in it next week, and stay a day or two.'

Lady Eleanor's brow clouded; she gave
her son no sign that she had heard him, but
went on with what she was saying to Lord
Heathfield.

After a glance at his mother's face, Lionel
did not repeat his remark; he began to

whistle, and was fain to walk behind with Charles Hargrave, whose countenance, always rather melancholy, bore traces of extra depression.

As the party reached the house, Lady Eleanor drew Elsie aside and said confidentially, 'Lionel has invited some of his M'Nabs.'

'You don't say so!' said Elsie. 'How many?'

'Two,' said Lady Eleanor, 'a man and a woman. I shall give them the worst rooms in the house.'

CHAPTER IV.

'Of all the Highland clans
M'Nab is most ferocious ;
Except the M'Intyres,
M'Craws and M'Intoshes.'

THERE was a considerable element of truth
in the account which Lady Eleanor had given
to Elsie of her nieces. Both Constance and
Blanche were greatly changed since the days
when we first met them at Alkerton, whether
for the better or the worse it is difficult to
say. Since her marriage Constance Ferrars
had almost entirely laid aside her disagree-
ably supercilious manner ; on the other hand
she had become somewhat commonplace and
uninteresting. Her husband was one who
professed to admire good housekeeping in
his wife rather than good looks ; accordingly
Constance, neglecting her outward appear-

ance, threw her whole soul into the management of her house and servants. Though
she no longer cared to assert her superiority,
her sense of her own importance was by no
means lessened; hence her own affairs and
those of her husband formed her constant
theme of discourse, which was apt at times to
weary the patience of her friends.

It need hardly be said that Blanche was
no longer disposed to follow her sister's
lead, she would have been highly indignant
had it been suggested that she followed the
lead of any one; she had 'views' of her own,
and a soul which despised the ordinary lot of
women. Of men too she had a very poor
opinion, 'idle, selfish creatures,' she would
say, 'thinking of nothing but sport and
pleasure, and without any high feelings or
aspirations.' In spite, however, of her contempt for the male sex, Blanche liked admiration, of which she received a good share;
for though without regular features, she was
very handsome on a large scale, and looked
the picture of health and vigour. She was

now engaged to Mr. Charles Hargrave, who
was the eldest son of the managing partner
in the great brewing firm of Hopwood and
Hargrave, at Stourton, S——shire.   This
young gentleman had become attached to
Blanche perhaps from force of contrast; he
was gentlemanlike and refined in appearance,
and somewhat delicate in health, which lent
an air of interesting languor to his large blue
eyes, and slight, rather stooping figure.   He
was a kindly, well-disposed young man, not
perhaps overburthened with brains; and
Blanche had a real regard for him, though
few men would have borne as he did with all
her tempers and caprices.

Lady Eleanor troubled herself little about
her nieces and their affairs; she pursued
her own way, and was seldom seen in the
drawing-room before luncheon.   Elsie found
herself in continual demand; she had to
listen to Constance whenever Mr. Ferrars
did not claim his wife's attention; she held
long arguments with Blanche, and was the
repository of all that young woman's con-

fidences; she had to soothe Charles Hargrave
as often as he was driven to desperation by
his lady-love's ill-humour; and she had to
pay polite attention to Lord Heathfield, who
was always ready to give her instruction.
Amidst all these claims she had little time
to bestow on Lionel—poor Lionel, who had
grown so kind and gentle, and who waited
so patiently for his opportunities, now few
and far between, of speaking to her. Yes,
upon the whole Elsie was glad she had not
gone to Rossie; she was certainly of use to
Lady Eleanor, and all would yet go well.
Perhaps, after all, she had been mistaken
about Lionel; he did treat her much more
like a sister, and when he took her aside it
was to consult her about household matters,
or to plan some expedition for the entertain-
ment of his guests.

A few fine days alternated with many
wet ones, in which the ladies necessarily
remained a good deal indoors. The weather
had 'broken' earlier than usual, the in-
habitants said; but as this remark was

repeated every year about the same time, it had lost a little of its significance.

'Well, what have you been doing?' said Blanche, as two of the sportsmen came in, wet and rather dispirited, one afternoon.

The incessant rain was blowing in sheets past the window, blotting out the distant hills; upon the nearer ones hung an ominous little wreath of mist; the colours of sky, sea, and land seemed blurred and mixed together into one dull shade of gray. Blanche was sitting on a low seat by the fire, studying a book of Celtic inscriptions and antiquities of the neighbourhood, in order thoroughly to get up the subject, as it was proposed to make an excursion the first fine day to an old chapel on a neighbouring island.

'Where are the others?' she said, 'and how many grouse have you shot?'

'Lionel has not come in yet,' replied Charles Hargrave, stretching out his cold hands to the fire, 'and Heathfield has gone to change his clothes. We did not shoot grouse at all; we shot snipe and a few rabbits—did not you hear those shots as we came in ?'

'Douglas dear, do go and change your clothes,' said Constance, feeling her husband's trousers anxiously. 'You are wet through, and will certainly get a return of your lumbago.'

Mr. Ferrars departed, muttering some imprecations upon the climate, and Charley Hargrave was about to follow when Blanche detained him.

'Tell us something interesting,' said she, 'you are very dull company, after all. Did you shoot well ?'

'Not very,' was the reply. 'Three of us fired at the same rabbit as we came in—you must have heard the shots.'

'I am disappointed in you, Charles,' said Blanche, turning away. 'Why don't you kill things for yourself instead of shooting other people's dead rabbits ? Yes, you may go and change your clothes,' and Blanche resettled herself to her studies.

Presently the door opened again and in

came Lionel, with muddy boots and clothes
and hair glistening with raindrops, but with
an air of having enjoyed himself, quite
different from the other two.

'Lionel, don't sit down!' cried his mother,
suddenly starting up from her novel as her
son entered. 'You will ruin the furniture.'

Lionel glanced down at his wet clothes,
and stood with his back against the mantelpiece, smiling down upon the company
serenely. 'Is it near dinner-time?' said he.
'The intelligent observer may discover, even
in this room, that we are going to have curry
for dinner.'

'You need not tell us that, Lionel,' said
Lady Eleanor crossly. 'Have we not been
sitting here smelling it the whole afternoon?
There is nothing more disgusting than a
house which smells of cooking.'

No one had observed the odour until
Lionel opened the door, but at these words
each one sniffed the air and shook his or
her head mournfully; Constance alone smiled
a contented smile. 'Douglas likes curry,'

she murmured. 'Aunt Eleanor, *where* do you get your curry-powder?'

Lady Eleanor turned her eyes vacantly upon Constance and answered, 'I'm sure I don't know, my dear. Lionel, how your clothes smell of rabbits and—dogs! Why are you not like your cousin Basil? he went and changed directly—and here he is,' as Lord Heathfield, looking particularly clean and dry, walked in, and, placing himself on a comfortable chair by Elsie's side, began to converse with her about poetry in a low voice. Lionel eyed his cousin with as much contempt as he was capable of calling into his countenance; and his mother was again about to make some remark when she was interrupted by Constance, whose mind was still running upon Indian condiments.

'Douglas used to get a box of curry-powder and chutney and sauces direct from India every year. He got it through a friend, and now—is it not provoking?—the friend is dead, so he can't get any more. Where do you advise me to go? You can't get those things thoroughly good at the Army and Navy.'

'How does the sea affect you?' inquired Heathfield of Elsie.

'It only affects me when it is rough,' she answered, wondering why Lord Heathfield should pause in the middle of a poetical discourse to ask her if she was liable to sea-sickness.

Heathfield looked a little puzzled. 'To me,' he said, 'it appeals at all times. The violence of the storm, the boom of the waves on a rock-bound shore, may stir up strong emotion; yet even in tranquillity it is ever varied. Do you remember those lines of Wordsworth—

> "The gentleness of heaven is on the sea;
> Listen! the mighty being is awake,
> And doth with his eternal motion make
> A sound like thunder—everlastingly."'

'Oh yes! I understand,' said Elsie. 'I thought you meant—oh yes! I do prefer a calm infinitely, every one must, I think, who has lived by the sea, and who really knows it.'

'Why don't you write poetry yourself, Heathfield?' said Lionel sarcastically. 'A sonnet now—on the sea by moonlight—a most original subject; or an ode to Punctuality.'

'Don't tease him, Lionel,' said Blanche, in a tone of elder-sisterly admonition.

'Well, I'll go and change,' said Lionel, feeling that Heathfield, who was allowed to sit down, had decidedly the best of it; and he departed, while Elsie's eyes followed him wistfully. He had come in so pleasant and cheerful, and everybody had snubbed him; and now he had gone away displeased, and probably would not get over it the whole evening, and though a kind word from her would put him right, it would be better not to speak it; he might think—he might fancy she meant more—and once again Elsie heartily wished herself at home.

The rain beat and the wind howled all night; and the next morning there was no change in the prospect.

The M'Nabs will never come in such

weather,' said Elsie soothingly to Lady Eleanor.

'They are capable of anything,' returned her hostess gloomily.

The gentlemen of the party did not go out that morning; they remained, some in the drawing-room, and some in the smoking-room, according to their several tastes. Mr. Fitzgerald and Lady Eleanor retired to the library; Constance disappeared at a call from her husband; Lionel came into the drawing-room, but finding that Heathfield had established himself in his favourite chair, and proposed to read aloud to the ladies, he withdrew sulkily, and was presently seen going out, solitary, in the rain.

Charley Hargrave also came into the drawing-room, and sat waiting, rather impatiently, for the reading to cease, that he might talk to Blanche, and looking out of the window. A sudden exclamation from him made everybody look up.

'Actually a vessel on the loch! Can that be the M'Nabs' yacht?'

There could be no doubt about it ; it was
a large steam yacht, and was making straight
for the landing-place.   Lionel had seen it
also, and had gone down to the shore.   Elsie
was on her way to tell Lady Eleanor when
she caught sight of Neil, the page-boy,
hurrying up from the shore, and went to
meet him.

'What is it, Neil ? have Mr. and Miss
M'Nab come ?'

' Please, ma'am, I was to tell her ladyship
that they will be come, and four more pair-
sons forbye.'

'What ?' said Elsie, in great consternation.
' Tell me who are come, Neil.'

' There will be Captain M'Nab and Mistress M'Nab, and young Mr. M'Nab and
three young ladees, and they will aal be
wushin' to sleep in the hoose,' replied Neil,
appearing to breathe more freely after he had
delivered his message without a mistake.

Elsie broke the news to Lady Eleanor as
best she might.   It was perfectly true ; six
dripping forms were presently seen accom-

panying Lionel up the approach, followed at a little distance by two more, who proved to be a lady's-maid and a piper, without whom the M'Nabs never stirred abroad.

'But it is monstrous!' said Lady Eleanor. 'It is incredible! I cannot have them in the house. Frederick, do you not see those people? Go out at once—quick, and tell them to go away.'

'But, my dear Eleanor, it—it is raining.'

'Never mind the rain! go at once—go quickly and speak to them.'

Mr. Fitzgerald went helplessly to the door; Elsie followed him with an umbrella.

'Lady Eleanor will be quite glad to see them,' she said, 'but please make a sign to Lionel to speak to us.'

Mr. Fitzgerald only groaned, but was presently seen shaking hands all round with apparent cordiality.

In another minute Lionel darted in. 'Mother, this is rather an invasion,' said he hastily; 'but you will be able to put them up somehow? They were on their way south, and were driven in by the storm. We must keep them till it is over.'

'Put them up!' said Lady Eleanor. 'It is perfectly impossible to put them up, Lionel, and I don't know what you mean—you are most inconsiderate. You must go and tell them I won't have them in the house.'

'But you *must* have them in the house,' said Lionel, with decision. 'One could not turn a dog out of doors in such weather; and they are wet through.' He glanced at Elsie, who came forward.

'Lady Eleanor, I am sure we could manage,' she said. 'I have been thinking it over, and you shall have no trouble. I could sleep with Blanche——'

'And two of them could sleep in the library,' put in Lionel unluckily.

'They can *not* sleep in the library,' retorted his mother, turning upon him. 'Is the house to be made into a pig-sty because a company of—mountebanks choose to arrive in a yacht?'

'I don't know, and it doesn't matter,' said

Lionel, doggedly.   'Somebody can have my
room of course ; but to talk of sending them
away is common nonsense.   Come, mother.'

'Well, it is your house, do as you please
of course,' said Lady Eleanor suddenly.
'Elsie, I leave it to you since you seem so con-
fident ; it is quite beyond me, I confess,' and
her ladyship walked with dignity to the door.

The guests had by this time reached the
hall, and were stripping off their saturated
cloaks and greatcoats.   Captain M'Nab,
who had got rid of his, quickly advanced with
a bow.

'Indeed I consider this a most fortunate
meeting ; I am delighted to make your acquaintance, Lady Eleanor,' he said, in answer
to her polite expressions of regret at their
half-drowned condition.   'My wife '—indicat-
ing a middle-aged lady in a billycock hat and
an ulster—'my daughters—Miss Williams,
my daughters' charming friend—and my son
Roderick.   I fear our numbers must have
taken you by surprise, but my friend Lionel
would take no refusal.'

'I told you we were intruding, Hector,' said Mrs. M'Nab, who looked very cross.

'No intrusion in the world,' said Lady Eleanor, 'I am only sorry that our room is limited.'

'Oh, we are easily accommodated,' cried Captain M'Nab. 'I was sure you would be delighted to see us—I told my wife so. Highland hospitality, you know.'

Here Elsie and Lionel came in together, and suggested dry clothes, an offer which was gladly accepted by all. The luggage not having been brought up from the yacht, Blanche and Elsie were obliged to ransack their wardrobes for garments in which to array their guests, and Lady Eleanor sent her own maid with a dress for Mrs. M'Nab, which was however declined, as that lady's strong ulster had protected her tolerably well. Elsie had given up her room to accommodate the Misses M'Nab, and the girls assembling there, a general trying on of dresses took place.

It was impossible to be stiff or disdainful

under the circumstances, and even Blanche joined in the laughter. Miss Ethel Williams, who was extremely small and fairy-like in figure, looked very comical in one of Elsie's dresses, which was much too long for her. Annie M'Nab, who was middle-sized and commonplace, was able to put on another, although it was rather tight; while Flora, the elder sister, a stout, handsome, broad-shouldered girl, managed, after great difficulty, to struggle into one belonging to Blanche, not without a considerable loss of buttons and hooks.

'It is too bad,' said Blanche, as she and Elsie repaired to the room they were to share together, 'to have them bursting all our best gowns. Did you ever see such a collection of monsters?'

'What *shall* we do with them?' said Elsie disconsolately, looking out of the window at the rain.

'Never mind them just now — they seem very well able to take care of themselves. What do you think of them,

Elsie? what is your opinion of your country-women?'

'Mrs. M'Nab is not my countrywoman,' said Elsie quickly; 'I am sure she is English by her voice. But the girls—how exactly like her father Miss Flora is. I daresay *some* people might call her handsome.'

'She has a good deal of side on,' said Blanche. 'Did you see how she squares her elbows? The other one is nothing at all.'

'No, she is plain, though I like her face better than her sister's. But that little Miss Williams is pretty, very piquant-looking; she is a Welsh girl, Lionel says.'

'Did Lionel appear to take much interest in her?' inquired Blanche drily. 'I *thought* I saw her rolling her eyes whilst he was helping her off with her coat.'

'Oh, I daresay she is quite that sort of girl,' said Elsie. 'Luckily, there are a good many young men here, so that she will be amused.'

'If she thinks we are going to lend her our young men to roll her eyes at, as well as our clothes to spoil, she will find herself very much mistaken,' said Blanche indignantly. 'Just you keep your eye on Lionel, Elsie, and stand no nonsense—that is my advice.'

'But I want Lionel to marry; I would like him to fall in love with some nice girl,' said Elsie earnestly.

'Do you want him to fall in love with Ethel Williams before your very eyes? answer me that.'

'No, I don't.'

'I thought not. Not that I think there is much danger of it,' said Blanche kindly, 'but "Highland hospitality" may be carried too far. We shall have to go down—there is the gong for luncheon.'

CHAPTER V.

'You shall not exist
  For another day more ;
I will shoot you, sir,
  Or stab you with my claymore ! '

THE M'Nabs did not take long to make
themselves at home, and were disposed to be
pleasant and talkative. Captain M'Nab,
who had been a naval officer, was a lively,
energetic little man, youthful-looking and
rather handsome. He was full of good
humour, praised the dishes at table, com-
plimented his hostess, and poured forth one
anecdote after another for the enlivenment of
the company. His wife was severe, not to
say forbidding in appearance; she spoke
little, her eyes were constantly upon her
daughters; she was civil to Lady Eleanor
and smiled upon Lionel, but snubbed Blanche

or Elsie as often as they ventured to speak
to her.   Her son was a heavy-looking youth
of seventeen or eighteen ; he spoke no word,
good or bad, but stared at Ethel Williams
with light blue lack-lustre eyes.   Flora
M'Nab was frank and handsome, affecting a
gentlemanly deportment ; she leaned back in
her chair, laughed loudly, and used a good
many slang words.   Ethel Williams, on the
contrary, complained of fatigue, spoke in a
faint voice, and refused to eat ; but was not
too much exhausted to carry on a low-toned
conversation with her next neighbour, Lord
Heathfield, to whom she lifted her beautiful
appealing eyes in a way which made havoc
in the heart of that susceptible young noble-
man.

The afternoon passed rather heavily ; the
guests sat round, looking at one another and
at their hosts as if they expected some enter-
tainment to have been provided, but none
was forthcoming.   Lady Eleanor, with her
stateliest air, was making conversation to
Mrs. M'Nab ; Constance Ferrars retired to

her room ; Blanche buried herself in a book,
and took no notice of any one ; Elsie alone
was affected by the depression of her guests.
To raise their spirits she told them that a
servants' ball was in preparation in the barn
for the following evening, and that all would
be expected to dance at it ; but as to-morrow
night was in the distance, this news was received with only a faint show of interest.

Flora M'Nab jumped up noisily, squared
her elbow and pointed her toe as if about to
dance ; then catching Ethel Williams round
the waist, she began to whistle the tune of
a schottische, and to prance about. Lady
Eleanor turned her head with an expression
of dignified surprise, and the girls stopped,
feeling uncomfortable. Elsie proposed some
music.

'Oh! I wonder if Ethel's fiddle has come
up from the yacht,' said Flora. 'Just run
and see, Annie, will you ?'

Annie went obediently, and Flora, sitting
down to the piano with a yawn, began to
play a waltz, carelessly, and with a good

many wrong notes. She broke off abruptly
in the middle.

'I have forgotten the rest,' she said, 'and
I have not got my music. Oh! dear me'—
with another yawn—'can you play, Miss Ross?'

'No, I am sorry I can't,' replied Elsie.
'Are you fond of music?'

Flora only nodded, and Ethel Williams,
turning up her eyes, said 'I adore it.'

'Blanche, do come and sing us something,'
said Elsie.

'Sing? oh, don't ask me, Elsie. One
cannot sing to order, and I am not in the
humour just now.'

'Here, Ethel, is your violin,' said Annie
entering. 'I hope it has taken no harm—
the case was rather wet.'

Ethel received it in silence; she seldom
wasted words upon her own sex. She opened
the case, took out the instrument, and began
to tune it, making such excruciating sounds
that Blanche and Elsie were tempted to put
their fingers in their ears, and Lady Eleanor
felt that this was not to be borne.

'Would you rather we went into the library, Mrs. M'Nab?' said she.

Mrs. M'Nab replied that she was quite comfortable where she was.

'It is unfortunate,' said Lady Eleanor, rising, 'but I have a dislike—a constitutional dislike, to hearing a violin tuned. We cannot account for or control those nervous feelings. But pray remain here if you prefer it.'

Mrs. M'Nab thought it best to follow, and the two ladies retired to the library. Blanche presently beat a retreat to her own room, and after what seemed to Elsie an interminable time the gentlemen came in and the strangers began to recover something like animation. Lord Heathfield at once made his way to Miss Williams's side; and Lionel, sitting down to the piano, played till tea was announced, and they all adjourned to the library. Afterwards, the rain having ceased, he proposed a walk, which was agreed to with alacrity, only Lord Heathfield and Miss Williams preferring to remain indoors.

It transpired during the walk that the M'Nab party intended to stay at Ardvoira till Saturday, the day of their arrival being Thursday. Captain M'Nab again made some slight apology for their numbers.

'But,' said he, 'the weather is more likely to be settled by Saturday, and now we are in such good quarters I—I assure you we are in no hurry to move. The more the merrier, eh, Lionel? and I am sure no one could have better fare.'

Lionel, who had to sleep in the yacht, was not particularly overjoyed at the prospect of spending two nights there; however, he entreated Captain M'Nab to consult his own convenience entirely, which that gentleman, with much earnestness, pledged himself to do. He walked alongside of Lionel, and confided to him many interesting particulars respecting his family.

'It is curious,' said he, 'but my wife now —she is of no birth—none at all.'

'Indeed!' said Lionel. 'You astonish me.'

Captain M'Nab regarded him sternly.

'Naturally,' said he, 'you are surprised. Had I considered my personal feelings—but I sacrificed them to duty. I trampled them under foot.'

'What circumstances,' asked Lionel, maintaining his gravity by an effort, 'could have made such a duty necessary?'

'Ah, my young friend, you may well ask! The M'Nabs were not what they once were. Our lands have been taken from us—at least they would have been, if I had not——'

'Married Mrs. M'Nab?' suggested Lionel.

'Auchenbothie Castle, which has been the stronghold of our race for centuries, the islands of Meish and Neish in the Outer Hebrides—every acre of land I have left would have gone to the hammer if I had not taken this—unusual, perhaps—but this decided step; if I had not, to put it in plain words, married a Birmingham pin-girl, and not even a good-looking one!'

Lionel, overwhelmed with admiration of this noble deed, was unable for the moment to make any reply. Presently he said, 'It has been a case of virtue its own reward, no doubt.'

Captain M'Nab paused to hit off the head of a thistle with his stick, then, wheeling round upon his companion, he answered, 'You are right; I have never had cause to repent it. My wife is an excellent woman, and perfectly well-bred. Her children take after my side of the house; they were brought up on principles of my own. I never allowed my girls to wear stays until they were grown up—you see the result.'

'Astonishing!' said Lionel, raising his eyes to look at the 'results,' who were some paces on in front.

'When my daughter Flora first entered a ballroom,' pursued the captain, 'there was a general rush, then a perfect scramble for introductions. We were taken for brother and sister.'

'Probably twins,' murmured Lionel.

At this Captain M'Nab darted a sharp look at him, but observing the extreme, almost mournful gravity of the young man's countenance, he continued—

'The Prince of Wales once said of her, "That is a deuced handsome girl." It was at a review; I did not hear it myself; it was repeated to me; but I can believe it, eh?'

'Certainly,' said Lionel.

'It is pretty to see her with the little Williams,' said Captain M'Nab. 'A charming girl, Lionel; charming, that is, for a southron. We would not care about such small figures in our clan. In the old times, when the M'Nabs were in their glory, a girl of that size would have been put to death without mercy; she would never have been suffered to grow up. Well, well, the old days were rough after all.'

The gallant captain continued for some time to dilate upon young ladies and their charms, and Blanche and Elsie came in for a due share of commendation; but when the latter was mentioned Lionel made some excuse to leave him, and walked on with the ladies.

With the assistance of music and games the evening passed gaily, until, the elder gentlemen coming in from the smoking-room, a party of whist was made up. Mr. Fitzgerald, who piqued himself on his skill in the game, had Douglas Ferrars for his partner, while Constance played with Captain M'Nab. Soon Lady Eleanor and Mrs. M'Nab, who were sitting together on the sofa, were startled by a somewhat noisy dispute at the whist-table, which ended in the fiery captain springing up, throwing his cards on the table, and exclaiming, 'I decline to play any longer! After such an accusation, I decline it utterly and entirely!'

'What is the matter?' asked Lady Eleanor.

'Hector, I am ashamed of you,' said Mrs. M'Nab. 'To lose your temper over a *game!*'

'What *is* the matter?' said Lady Eleanor again.

'A case of revoke!' cried Mr. Fitzgerald, who also appeared considerably heated,—

'a clear case of revoke! You refused spades
—you all saw him refuse spades,' he continued, looking round,—'and look here!' He
caught up the hand of cards from the table
and triumphantly produced the seven of
spades.

'Do you wish to insult me?' shouted the
captain, dancing with rage. 'I decline to
submit—I—I leave this house to-morrow!'
and he seemed about to bolt out of the
room, when Lady Eleanor interfered.

'Captain M'Nab,' said she, 'I am sure
no rudeness was intended. Frederick, who
cares for your trumpery seven of spades?
Put it away and be quiet. Tell Captain
M'Nab you did not mean to be offensive.'

'I certainly hope that no one will leave
my son's house,' said Mr. Fitzgerald; 'but
as to the revoke, it was a palpable one.'

Lady Eleanor waved her hand impatiently; but Captain M'Nab had by this
time recovered himself. 'Lady Eleanor,'
said he magnanimously, 'I am hot-blooded
—I admit it; it is a characteristic of my

race.   But one word from a lady, and I am disarmed.   Let us say no more about this occurrence; I am willing that it should be forgotten.'

Lady Eleanor bowed, so did Mr. Fitzgerald, and a rather awkward silence ensued; then the hostess, discovering that it was more than time to retire, desired Lionel to light the bedroom candles, and forced away the unwilling young party from their game.

'That Captain M'Nab is the most detestable man,' said Constance the next morning.   'Just fancy, Aunt Eleanor, Douglas said he was *so* rude to him last night in the smoking-room.'

'He is a quarrelsome little creature,' returned her aunt indifferently.   'People should not irritate him.   What was it all about?'

'Oh, they got upon politics, and he said the most dreadful things!   He thinks all Radicals should be hanged, and wishes Mr. Gladstone to be drawn and quartered.'

'There would not be many people left

in Scotland if his wishes were carried out,'
said Lady Eleanor drily.

'And Douglas did not irritate him,'
continued Constance in an injured tone.
'Douglas is not a Radical, you know—he
is an advanced Liberal, and his opinion
was——'

'And what more did Captain M'Nab do
or say ?' interrupted her aunt.

'Oh, he was most insulting about that
horrid election at Slumborough last year.
You know Douglas not getting in was entirely the result of bribery.'

'And did they come to blows ?'

'Aunt Eleanor, please do not laugh at it ;
Douglas might have been killed.   Captain
M'Nab was gesticulating with a soda-water
bottle—just fancy if it had struck him !—
but Lionel gave his arm a little jerk and
he let it fall, and mercifully it broke on the
floor.'

'Well, it is very tiresome,' said Lady
Eleanor ; 'the carpet will be full of broken
glass.   I wish the M'Nabs would go away,

with all my heart, and what I am to do about Heathfield I don't know, for the silly boy seems quite infatuated with that Miss Williams.   The charge of a young man is a heavy responsibility.'

This conversation took place before breakfast, Lady Eleanor and Constance being the first in the dining-room; it was interrupted by Lord Heathfield's entrance, and his aunt did not fail to notice that he wore in his buttonhole a pink carnation which had adorned Miss Williams's dress the evening before.

There was a marked improvement in the weather that day; the gentlemen made preparations to go out to shoot, and Lady Eleanor called her son aside.

'Lionel,' she said, 'remember that I trust to you to take care of Heathfield.   He is making a perfect fool of himself with that Miss Williams—his parents would be dreadfully annoyed if they knew.'

'My dear mother, am I Heathfield's keeper?'

'There is no occasion to be profane. Take him out with you to shoot, and keep him with you—that is all I ask. Don't listen to any of his excuses.'

'I can't take him if he doesn't want to go. Besides, I don't know that we can all shoot.'

'Then leave some one else behind—leave the M'Nab boy.'

'The M'Nab boy is going to fish, and Heathfield said something about it too.'

'I won't have Heathfield fish,' cried Lady Eleanor vehemently; 'he will loiter about the house the whole day long. Can't you make some excuse? Leave Douglas Ferrars behind and take Heathfield—tell him you are afraid of Douglas and Captain M'Nab shooting each other.'

Lionel burst out laughing. 'A brilliant idea, mother! I *will* tell him so—it will be a great joke. Heathfield believes everything I tell him if I am only solemn enough.'

'Do not be silly and make a jest of every-thing, Lionel,' said his mother. 'I would not have you tell an untruth for the world. They really might shoot one another—at least Captain M'Nab might shoot Douglas. Not that he would be any great loss,' she added meditatively.

'Nevertheless it is our duty, as Christians, to prevent bloodshed,' said Lionel. 'Besides, I do not wish to be annoyed with his funeral. Make your mind easy, mother; Heathfield shall go out shooting, and I have asked Major James and Mr. Fairlie to come to-night for the barn dance, so Miss Williams will have plenty of cavaliers.'

While the above conversation was going on, Flora M'Nab had laid hands upon her young brother and forcibly dragged him into the passage.

'Roddy, I want to speak to you.'

'What do you want?' grunted the unwilling Roderick.

'I want to ask you—papa does not really mean to go away to-day, does he?'

'I am sure I don't know. Can't you ask him yourself?'

'Don't be stupid! it would only put it into his head. He mustn't go till after the dance. I only mean, is he offended with Mr. Fitzgerald still?'

'No—I don't know. There was a row in the smoking-room last night.'

'With Mr. Fitzgerald?'

'No, not him, he went to bed—the other man.'

'Who? tell me quick.'

'Don't claw a fellow. Take away your hand or I'll not tell you anything.'

'Oh, bother! There, I'm not touching you. Who, Roddy?'

'The one with the bald head, I don't know his name.'

'Oh! and you think he'll stay?'

'I don't know and I don't care. Let me away, or I'll get him to go.'

'*You* get him to go indeed!' said Flora contemptuously, for her mind was now quite relieved. 'What are you going to do to-day, Roddy?'

'Fish,' replied Roderick laconically.

'Not shoot?'

'I'm not going to be bothered with all of *them.*'

'But you will have Lord Heathfield if you are going to fish; he said he was going to——'

'I don't want him, he's a fool. Get out of my way, can't you?' and, pushing his sister aside, Roderick went to collect his fishing tackle.

Captain M'Nab said nothing about leaving Ardvoira that day. There had been a slight cloud upon his brow at breakfast; he glared across the table at Douglas Ferrars, who glared back again, but no word passed between them. Lionel did not fail to remind Heathfield of this circumstance, and by his artful representations so worked upon the guileless mind of that excellent young man that he consented to join the shooting party, while Mr. Ferrars was invited by the ladies to drive with them to Glen Torran.

Lady Eleanor had intended that Ethel Williams should accompany her thither, but

the young lady excused herself on the plea
that driving always gave her a headache;
and all the girls of the party begged to be
allowed to stay at home and decorate the
ballroom. This occupied them the most of
the day, and in the afternoon they received
assistance from the sportsmen, who came in
from shooting rather early. The work, however, proved too exhausting for some of the
party, and when Lady Eleanor returned
from her drive she found her nephew and
Miss Williams in their accustomed corner of
the drawing-room, apparently quite satisfied
with themselves and their position.

CHAPTER VI.

'I am sham'd thro' all my nature to have lov'd so slight a thing.'

MAJOR JAMES and Mr. Fairlie were two gentlemen who rented Loch Voira Lodge, a shooting on the other side of the loch, and were pretty frequent visitors at Ardvoira. Major James was a stout, middle-aged man, with a good-natured face and twinkling eyes. He had a fund of quiet humour, a love of the good things of this life, and was a keen observer without seeming to be so. His friend Mr. Fairlie was a much younger man; he was fond of sport and somewhat shy in ladies' society.

Immediately after dinner the whole party adjourned to the barn, which was a large one, and had been built by old Mr. Macdonald with a view to entertainments of this

sort. The night was fine but dark, Lady
Eleanor called for a lantern, and with some
difficulty one was procured, and care had to
be taken not to stray off the farm road or
fall into the ditch.

The barn when they arrived, however,
was tolerably well lighted with candles and
a few Chinese lanterns. One by one they
ascended the winding wooden stair; the
buzz of talking ceased, and every one stood
up as they came in. Some seats had been
erected at one end of the room, and as soon
as the elders of the party were settled in
their places Lionel spoke apart to the
musicians, who consisted of the M'Nabs'
piper; Pritchard, who was a performer on
the violin; and several other amateurs in
the neighbourhood. The pipers struck up a
reel, and every one who could dance it was
soon in motion. The ballroom was somewhat crowded, and to a spectator the mass
of moving figures was bewildering and the
noise deafening, for the music was mingled
with the sound of stamping, shouts, and yells.

Captain M'Nab particularly distinguished himself; he leaped higher, stamped harder, yelled louder, and snapped his fingers more sonorously than any one else in the room; all animosity seemed to be forgotten.

The first dance was not permitted to be exclusive, every one took a partner from among the farm or house servants, but when it ended Lionel looked about for Elsie. She was sitting down, and he made his way to her at once.

'You not dancing, Elsie? I thought you were famous at reels. You will dance the next with me, won't you? it is a schottische.'

'I have been sitting out this dance with my partner,' explained Elsie, as she rose and took Lionel's arm; 'he is the fisherman from Loch Voira, and a very agreeable man; but he tells me he can't dance because he has sprained his leg to-morrow fortnight. He hass not fery much English.'

'I am in luck to get you for this, I suppose,' said Lionel, as he led her out; 'I never see you now, Elsie. Why do you avoid me as if I had got some disease?'

'Lionel, don't say that. We must do our duty, you know, to the company; I don't think we are doing it now.'

'Nonsense! this is the dance when we are all allowed to choose our partners; look at Heathfield figuring away with Miss Williams.'

'Yes—come, Lionel, don't let us lose it all; I love a schottische.'

It was a pretty sight to see Elsie dance; so lightly, and with such evident enjoyment, and yet with a sort of measured grace which prevented the possibility of turning the Highland schottische into the romp which it is too apt to become. So thought Lady Eleanor as she watched the pair approvingly, but Mrs. M'Nab turned up her nose.

'Miss Ross has just come from abroad, has she not? She seems to affect a sort of French manner.'

'Frenchwomen *do* know how to carry themselves, don't they?' answered Lady

Eleanor. 'Young ladies nowadays so often dance like dairymaids,' and her eye rested on Flora; 'but Elsie did not learn her manners in France.'

The order of the dances generally consisted in two reels and then a waltz for the benefit of the gentlefolks, and after every two or three dances a Gaelic song was called for. The singer had no musical accompaniment, but every one who knew the chorus joined in; while the audience sat in a ring round the room, and every two persons waved a pocket-handkerchief between them, each holding it by a corner, and swaying it gently to and fro in time to the music, according to the Highland custom. After the first two or three dances Lady Eleanor left, accompanied by her husband, the Ferrarses, and Mrs. M'Nab, but the others remained till a pretty late hour. Liberal refreshments had been provided for the dancers down below, but the 'quality' refrained from partaking of these in view of the supper which awaited them at home. At last even the stout-limbed

M'Nabs showed symptoms of weariness;
and, after Lionel had made a short speech,
which was received with much applause,
the party withdrew amidst tumultuous and
renewed cheering.

There was no lantern this time to guide
their steps, and Lionel, drawing Elsie's arm
within his, went on in front, feeling his way
cautiously.

'Let every man give his arm to a lady and
follow,' said he. 'It won't do to fall into that
ditch.'

For the last hour or so it had been remarked by Major James, who had been more
of a spectator than an actor, that Lord
Heathfield had disappeared, and that Miss
Williams, whether from fatigue or some
other cause, was looking pale and unhappy.
In coming down the wooden stair she called
out that she had twisted her foot. Several
gentlemen proposed to carry her home, but
she declined these offers, and managed to
walk, supported on each side by Major James
and his friend.

'Are we all in?' cried Lionel as they reached the door.

'Wait one moment,' said Major James. 'There is a lady seriously hurt.'

'Miss Williams! what have you done to yourself?' exclaimed Lionel, as the fair burden was brought into the dining-room and deposited in the largest arm-chair.

All crowded round with remedies, Lionel brought her a glass of wine, Charley Hargrave knelt down to take off her little shoe, and Captain M'Nab pinched her leg to see if any bones were broken.

'All sound, thank heaven!' said he with a serious face, addressing the company generally. 'In cases like this, always feel the limb first, to see if any bones are broken. When we were stationed at Zanzibar, a friend of mine slipped and broke his leg—bone was broken clean through, and he never would have known it if I had not pointed it out to him. I bandaged it at once—made him a pair of splints of two stout leaves of the aloe plant—bound it up with cocoa-nut matting—

had him carried to the ship by a couple of blacks—and in a very few weeks that man was on his legs again. The ship's doctor said no surgeon could have done it better. But this is a simple sprain, if Miss Ross happens to have any — where is Miss Ross ?'

Elsie had brought in a little iron kettle ; mended up the decaying fire, and at this moment entered with a pair of bellows.

' If it is a sprain,' said she, ' hot water——'

' Ah, that is the thing !' said Major James, taking the bellows from her, and blowing up the fire. ' We shall soon have Miss Williams all right.'

' *Hot* water, my dear Miss Ross !' cried Charles Hargrave in great excitement. ' When I sprained my ankle, I was ordered to have a continual trickle of cold water upon it night and day !'

' Let us carry Miss Williams into the pantry, and hold her foot under the cock !' suggested Lionel.

' But she could not stay there all night,

could she?' said Mr. Fairlie, giving his opinion with diffidence.

'Tight bandages to keep down inflammation!' said somebody else.

'That would only increase it!' shouted another.

'Arnica!' cried Captain M'Nab, raising his voice. 'Flora! Annie! have you brought any?'

By this time the water was hot, and Elsie, with Major James's assistance, bathed the patient's foot with it.

'Thank you,' she said faintly, 'I do think it feels better.'

Lionel drew in a little table, and supplied her with refreshments, saying, 'You must eat, Miss Williams, starvation is the worst thing in the world for a sprain.'

'There is nothing whatever the matter with her,' muttered Blanche, following Elsie as she went to replace the kitchen-bellows; 'look at all those men round her! is it not enough to make one sick?'

'I don't think there is much the matter,'

said Elsie ; ' but what on earth has become
of Heathfield ? '

Blanche only shrugged her shoulders, and
they returned to the dining-room, where the
rest had begun to attack the substantial cold
supper.

' Oysters, by all that's glorious ! ' said
Major James. ' Do let me help somebody.
Miss Mortimer — Miss Ross, after your
errands of mercy ? '

' Have some ham with your turkey,' said
Lionel, ' I can recommend it. But surely we
are not all here—where is Heathfield ?'

' Gone to bed two hours ago,' replied
Charley Hargrave. ' Where is Roddy
M'Nab ? '

Every one looked around, and at last his
sister Annie said, ' I don't think Roddy left
the barn when we did.'

' He did not seem able to tear himself
away from Katie Gillies, the grieve's
daughter,' said Flora scornfully.

' Never mind him,' said his father, ' he'll
turn up, never fear.'

And in truth young Mr. M'Nab returned safely, in company with the servants, at about five in the morning.

'Elsie,' said Blanche, when the two retired for the night, 'I'm tired to death, aren't you? That girl, Ethel Williams, with her airs, is enough to make a saint ill—*did* you see them all taking off her shoe? Yes, you may laugh, Elsie, but Lionel was quite as ready with his advice as any of them. We shall have him at her feet next.'

'I don't think Lionel took a serious view of the case,' said Elsie, 'or Major James either.'

'But Charley did,' said Blanche vindictively; 'he got quite excited about it; upon my word, he grows stupider every day. Really men are the most despicable creatures! I have a great mind to go into a convent.'

With these words Blanche flung herself into bed and buried her head in the bedclothes, as if bidding adieu to the world and its vanities; only looking up again to remark,

'If to-morrow is a wet day and they don't
go, I shall remain in this bed until they do.'

Before Elsie got into bed, she threw open
the window and looked out, breathing a
fervent prayer that the day might be fine.
'If we have two more days of them,' she
thought, 'for they cannot go away on Sunday, I do not know what will become of us.'

It seemed a fairish night; the wind was
sighing softly in the trees; a faint gray light
was creeping up the sky. In the distance
she could just hear the regular wash of the
tide; all promised well for the morrow, and
Elsie slept peacefully. She had forgotten to
pull down the blind, and in the morning was
awakened by the sun, which streamed into
the little room; it was a joyful sight. It was
one of those rarely beautiful days which are
doubly welcome in the 'broken weather' of a
West Highland autumn. Elsie, who had
come down a little early for breakfast, went
to the door to enjoy the sunshine, and presently caught sight of Lord Heathfield,
pacing up and down with a most woebegone

countenance.   She went up and spoke to him, and soon the two were deep in conversation.   As the gong sounded for breakfast, and they turned to enter the house, Elsie looked up and caught sight of Ethel Williams's face at her window; she had evidently been watching them.   Soon afterwards she appeared in the dining-room, limping a little, but declaring that her foot was much better, and that there was nothing to prevent her leaving Ardvoira that day.   Every one was down in fairly good time; there was a bustle of preparation, polite speeches and good-byes.   Captain M'Nab hurried his party off as soon after breakfast as might be; and Lady Eleanor had the satisfaction of seeing the white sails of the yacht round the point, and vanish behind its projecting crags.

'Thank Heaven they are gone!' exclaimed Blanche piously, as she extended herself in the best arm-chair the room afforded. 'What shall we do, Elsie? let us celebrate the occasion in some way.'

'Come out for a walk, Blanche.   There

has not been such a fine day since you came,
and it is a pity to lose any of it.'

'A walk?' said Blanche. 'I suppose I
shall have to take to regular walks some time
or other. You know I am getting much
stouter—don't you think so?'

'Let us walk to the top of the hill then,
and see the view—that will be very good for
you.'

'How much thinner do you think it will
make me?' said Blanche, rising lazily, and
putting a hand on each side of her shapely
waist; 'that consideration is a good deal
more important to me than any view. Well,
come along, I'll get ready.'

The two girls were soon on their way up
the hill at the back of the house, which was
not very difficult of ascent. They passed first
by a little path through the wooded glen,
crossing the river by a bridge, then, opening
a rustic gate, they found themselves on the
dry sunny hillside. Autumn tints had begun
to appear unmistakably amongst the foliage;
the birches which fringed the river banks

had already turned yellow, and were shower-
ing their leaves into the brown water. The
lady-ferns had faded ; and on the hillside the
purple heather had turned brown, and the
bent grass golden.

> ' It is the time when flowers grow old,
>   And summer trims her mantle's fringe
>   With stray threads of autumnal gold.'

'Now that we are alone,' said Blanche,
'tell me about Heathfield. I saw you come
in with him this morning, and I have been
dying to ask you what has been the matter.
Surely Ethel Williams can't have snubbed
him ?'

'Oh no !' said Elsie, 'not she, but he has
made up his mind to renounce her. She has
told him a lie.'

'Dear ! how pleased Aunt Eleanor will
be ! How big a lie was it ? What was it
about ?'

'He had not time to go into it very
minutely, and it was a painful subject, but as
far as I could gather, it was about Morris's
poetry, which she declared she adored, and

afterwards he found out that she had never read a line of it.'

'And was that all? was that the cause of all his woe? was that why he went to bed last night at eleven o'clock, and came down this morning looking like a dying fish?' and Blanche kicked away a stone contemptuously.

'He never closed his eyes all night,' said Elsie a little tremulously. 'It's a shame to laugh, but really to think of poor Heathfield not sleeping a wink all night because Ethel Williams told a lie.'

'As if she ever, by any chance, spoke the truth,' said Blanche. 'I could not have believed even Heathfield would have been so idiotic. Now I understand his leaving the ball, but why did she sprain her ankle?'

'I think she really did twist it a little; you know her heels were very high, and I don't think any one gave her his arm down the stair.'

'They could not,' said Blanche indignantly, 'there was not room. But I should have thought the sprain had been an excuse to stay.'

'I think, poor girl,' said Elsie hesitating, 'that she thought Heathfield had told me about the lie, and she did not like to stay. She might think he was going to tell everybody in the house.'

'Hum,' said Blanche. 'I don't know, but at any rate it is not worth while going into all her petty motives. How narrow people's minds are — how contemptible! Now there was not one of all that set that one could have exchanged an idea with; and our own party are very little better. What do they think of but sport? slaughtering unfortunate grouse and hares and sea-trout?'

'Oh, I do not think that is fair! Now even poor Heathfield is full of ideas, although they may not be very shrewd ones; and Lionel is very clever when he chooses to give his mind to a thing; and Mr. Hargrave——'

'Don't talk to me about Charley Har-

grave unless you are going to abuse him.
Ideas! he has no more ideas than a tom-
cat!'

'He has no opportunity of expressing
them; you snub him every time he opens
his mouth.'

'He has not got them to express,' per-
sisted Blanche. 'I am not at all sure,' she
went on, 'that marriage is not altogether
a mistake. Look at Constance and what
she has become—to be sure one need not
sink so low as that; but all married women
that I ever saw are either wholly given up
to society, or they have fallen into a state
of drivelling imbecility over their children
and servants and housekeeping. Now an
unmarried woman can let her mind expand
and develop; she can cultivate higher and
more exalted thoughts—dear me, how steep
this is, Elsie! let us sit down and rest upon
those stones.'

Elsie laughed as she sat down beside
her. 'If you are going to cultivate these
ideas, Blanche, you must really take more

exercise. Nobody will believe you are all soul if you are stout.'

Blanche smiled good-humouredly. 'How do you manage to keep so slim, Elsie? you, who don't profess to be all soul. Ah, but I believe you have ideas you don't talk about, you sly creature! perhaps that is what makes you *simpatica* with me. But you were going to say something about Charley—now I should like to have your real unbiassed opinion about him.'

'I like him,' said Elsie. 'I think him good and kind, dear Blanche, and a gentleman. And I am sure he really loves you.'

Blanche pulled up a handful of grass and looked at it attentively. 'Yes,' she said after a moment; 'I think he is all you say, but—you know his relations are all brewers; he is a brewer himself; I should have to live in a flat country (which I am not accustomed to), full of factories, and I should be utterly steeped and saturated in beer. Of course I mean morally. Well, there is not much soul in that, you will allow.'

'On the contrary, if you give up what you like, not from any mean motive, but for the sake of some one you care for, you would be doing a fine thing, and surely actions are better than ideas.'

'Well, but I might sink and become debased, and you have no idea how flat the country is—you can scarcely imagine it here,' and she looked pensively at the landscape. 'There really is a good deal of soul about these islands and hills and things. Come! I have a great mind to go to the top after all.'

They set themselves once more to the ascent, and in another quarter of an hour had reached the top of the hill.

'Look, Blanche!' said Elsie, pointing to a little speck far away on the blue water. 'I believe that is the M'Nabs' yacht. What ages it seems since they went!'

'I hope I shall never see them again,' said Blanche viciously. 'After all, wherever one lives, one is sure to have tiresome neighbours. I had forgotten the M'Nabs, and was just thinking of the delightful solitude of this place compared to Stourton. The people there are all so dull, and oh! my dear, if you only saw their clothes! Well, I suppose it is my fate,' and Blanche sighed deeply. From Blanche's manner, Elsie felt more sure than she had ever done before of the reality of her affection for Charles Hargrave; she had wondered at times whether Blanche was only playing with him, and felt sorry for the young man, whose gentle courtesy and forbearance she had often admired. She rejoiced, therefore, to see how Blanche seemed to court the subject, and was willing to find fault with her lover in order to be contradicted.

'Stourton will leave off being a dull neighbourhood when you are in it, Blanche,' she said gaily. 'You have plenty of energy in you, and will be able to work reforms. Your destiny shall be to give a higher tone to the society, and put exalted ideas into the people's heads.'

'I am to elevate the people,' said Blanche,

'while Charley elevates the beer. To do him justice, he has done that partly already, for he has set his face against putting tobacco into it. Fate is a strange thing, Elsie; I wonder what will be yours?'

'I have no fate,' answered Elsie. 'I have not it in me to reform people; I can suffer, but I cannot fight; I can only go with the stream. One thing I know; I shall never marry.'

'*You* never marry!' exclaimed Blanche. 'What rubbish!'

'It was foretold me once,' said Elsie dreamily, 'by a woman who told fortunes by the hand—years ago. I did not believe it—then—— But come, Blanche, we must not spend our lives on the top of this hill. Let us go home, or the people down below will be dragging the river for us.'

'Or the loch,' said Blanche. 'That would keep them amused for some time.'

CHAPTER VII.

'God calleth preaching folly.   Do not grudge
To pick out treasure from an earthen pot.
The worst speak something good ; if all want sense,
God takes a text and preacheth patience.'

'WE are all going to church to-day,' said
Lady Eleanor in a resolute tone the next
morning. 'I will hear of no excuses. Last
Sunday it was the rain which kept you away,
and the Sunday before it was something
else, but there can be no reason against
going to-day ;' and she pointed to the window, whence the sunshine streamed gaily in.

The weather had undoubtedly been a
sufficient excuse the Sunday before. Rain
had fallen in torrents, and not one of the
party had even ventured out of doors in the
morning. Instead, they had collected in the
drawing-room, and held some rather hot

arguments upon religious questions. The immortality of the soul had formed one of the chief subjects of dispute, and had given rise to a variety of opinions. Douglas Ferrars began by denying that the soul had any existence after death; he said he had reason for being quite convinced of the contrary, and could not be mistaken. His argument was, that he had once been very nearly drowned, in fact, quite insensible; and yet, spiritually, he had not experienced anything in particular.

Elsie advanced in reply, that being very nearly drowned is a different thing from being quite drowned, and that if the latter fate had overtaken Mr. Ferrars, he would not, at all events, have been able to come back and relate his experiences.

Mr. Ferrars was fond of telling the story of his escape from drowning, and it always made his wife very uncomfortable; she did not like to hear him putting forth heterodox opinions; neither did she like to hear him contradicted by Elsie.

'Douglas, dear, we are bound to accept the Church's teaching about a future life. But you know'—turning to Elsie, and speaking in a lowered tone—'he really was quite insensible and cold for two hours! They had three people to rub him, and five hot-water bottles before they could restore animation.'

'There, Elsie!' said Blanche, who had been listening; 'I am sure you will not insist upon Douglas's soul being immortal after that.'

'What is your opinion, Blanche?' asked Lionel. 'Let us have an exposition of your views. We are all attention.'

'I?' said Blanche. 'I am sure *my* soul is immortal; I do not answer for everybody's. I believe that people who cultivate very ignoble affinities, you know, are likely to be ultimately annihilated;' and she looked severely at Hargrave, who was tranquilly reading a yellow novel, and apparently took no interest in the discussion.

'We may find indications of an immortal

spirit,' said Heathfield thoughtfully, 'if we examine our own inner consciousness; and I think it would be impious to deny that there is a Divine spark, a germ of immortality, in every nature, however debased.'

'You are right, Basil,' said Lady Eleanor; 'of course there is; and I consider that this conversation is, as you say, impious. Any one would suppose we were all heathens. We ought to read the lessons for the day and a sermon—Frederick! why don't you read us a sermon?'

'Ahem—certainly,' replied Mr. Fitzgerald, without looking up from his paper.

Constance leaned back in her chair and took up her smelling-bottle; Heathfield and Charley Hargrave straightened their legs and solemnised their countenances; but Lionel made haste to change the subject. 'We must go to church at Loch Voira next Sunday,' he said; 'I should like to show you my improvements.'

Lionel had begun by stirring up the heritors to put a new roof upon the church,

and contributing largely himself for this purpose.   This done, it was soon discovered
that the walls needed painting, that the pews
were worm-eaten, and that the windows were
very inconvenient.   The old minister, Mr.
M'Phail, being of a liberal turn of mind, had
no objection to improvements or even inno-
vations; he saw no approach to 'Papistry'
in the stained window which was soon after
introduced, nor even in the harmonium which
was to supersede the worthy old precentor,
whose voice was beginning to give way; and he
was grateful to those of his congregation who
interested themselves in the 'improvement of
the psalmody' and the training of the choir.

Lionel, who took no small credit to himself for these improvements, seconded his
mother readily enough when, the next Sunday morning, she intimated her intention of
compelling her guests to attend public worship at Loch Voira.

'Some of you must walk to church,'
said Lady Eleanor, looking round, 'but
the carriage will hold five if necessary.'

'I would rather walk,' said Elsie.

'And I do not think I shall go at all,' said Constance.

'Not go to church this beautiful day, Constance!' said Lionel.

'Please say kirk, Lionel; it does sound so schismatical to talk of a Presbyterian Church. And I don't feel sure it is right to go.'

'But, Constance, "kirk" is every bit as good a word as "church,"' said Elsie, bristling up in defence of her native tongue, 'and means exactly the same thing.'

'And to say it is not right to go is positively absurd,' said Lady Eleanor, 'and sets a very bad example to the lower classes. When people come to Scotland they must do as the Ro— as others do. We cannot expect to have everything.'

'For my part,' said Blanche, 'I should make a point of attending the church of the country, whatever it might be. If I were in the East, I would worship in a mosque with pleasure.'

'You could not,' said Lionel, 'women are not allowed in mosques.'

'The Mahommedans,' observed Charley Hargrave, 'deny that women have souls, you must remember.'

'Then theirs is a most erroneous faith,' said Blanche, 'and I would not go into their mosques if they paid me for it. Elsie, if you are going to walk, I will walk with you —regular exercise, you know,' she added in an undertone as they left the room together.'

The two girls took a considerable time to arrange their Sunday bonnets to their satisfaction, and when they came downstairs, found only Lionel and Charley Hargrave waiting for them, the punctual Heathfield having walked on. Charley and Blanche went on in front, and Lionel stopped a moment to survey Elsie approvingly.

'You have put on your black dress to-day; I think I like it better than the white one; and how Sunday-like you look in that little bonnet! I think I should know by your face what day it was. Where do you get that expression, Elsie?'

'It is a Paris bonnet,' said Elsie hastily, 'perhaps that gives it. I can't compliment you on your Sunday appearance, Lionel.'

Lionel's billycock hat was pushed back off his forehead, and he was swinging a little cane. 'You ought to have walked with Heathfield,' he replied, 'there is a pious young man for you! Tall hat, kid gloves, and umbrella complete. Heathfield would be a good fellow,' he added, 'if he was not such an awful prig.'

'He *is* a good fellow,' said Elsie.

They talked of many things as they walked along, Elsie trying to steer clear of dangerous subjects, and establish a pleasant brotherly-and-sisterly footing between them, in which she began to think she had succeeded admirably. Lionel talked about his plans for the future, and told her he had some thoughts of letting Ardvoira and going away for a few years. A friend of his, who had settled in New Zealand, had asked him to go out there and see the country ; and it would be a good idea, he thought, to buy land there and set up a horse farm.

There was an affected carelessness in Lionel's manner when he told her this which did not escape Elsie, and she resolved to be on her guard.

'Do you approve of this plan ?' he said, suddenly turning and looking at her.

'Oh, Lionel, I should like you to travel, and to see places and people ; I think it is the best thing you could do. But to go to New Zealand—remember your mother has no one but you. And then a *horse* farm ! I never heard of a horse farm before—people in New Zealand have sheep farms, don't they ?'

'And why should *I* have a sheep farm ?' said Lionel in an offended tone. 'I suppose I may keep horses instead if I like—I understand them, I don't understand sheep—why, Elsie, you look quite shocked ! Is a sheep a more godly or virtuous animal than a horse, may I ask ? But'—he went on, suddenly laying aside his half-scornful tone as he saw her looking vexed—'if you tell me not to go, Elsie, there is an end of it. I don't want to go, goodness knows! and you could keep me here by one word.'

'I don't want to keep you here, Lionel,' said Elsie, in her most matter - of - fact manner, 'because I think travelling would be an excellent thing—it is only New Zealand and horse farming that I do not think advisable.'

'You would have me travel without an object then? anything to get me out of your sight, in short.'

Elsie made no answer, and they walked on a little way in silence, till, as they drew near the church and heard voices in the distance, Lionel felt that he could not afford to indulge in bad temper just then.

'Elsie, say something—I did not mean that, you know.'

She turned her sweet face towards him, smiling. 'No, don't let us quarrel just as we are going to church—let it be peace, Lionel.'

Lionel took her hand and held it as long as he dared, for in another few minutes they came in sight of their party, as well as the two gentlemen from the lodge, who, seated on the low wall of the churchyard, were awaiting the conclusion of the Gaelic service. Blanche had also with some difficulty hoisted herself upon the wall, and sat there looking rather dejected and very tired.

'Now, Miss Mortimer,' said Major James, when they had greeted the new-comers, 'have you no piece of information for us? Here we are all waiting to be improved—a few remarks upon these gravestones, now, would oblige the company.'

'Oh, don't ask me to preach you a sermon,' said Blanche; 'we shall have quite enough of that presently. Who is going to hold forth to-day?'

'A man of the name of Duff, from Aberbeenshire,' said Mr. Fairlie; 'he seems likely to be the successful candidate. You know they are appointing an assistant and successor to old M'Phail.'

'Well, I hope they won't appoint this man,' said Lionel; 'I've heard him, and I never want to hear him again. Ah! there is the Glen Torran waggonette,' and he went forward to open the door for Mrs. Carmichael, who just then drove up with her two little grandsons. The Ardvoira carriage next appeared, Mr. Fitzgerald and his wife being its only occupants; and now the Gaelic worshippers began to issue forth, while the cracked bell announced that the English service was shortly to begin.

'Would Constance not come after all?' asked Elsie as she joined Lady Eleanor.

'No, she made an excuse about Douglas having a headache, and said she was going to sit with him,' was the reply; 'but they may do as they please, *I* do not care whether they come or not.'

The jangling bell, whose sound was rendered yet more excruciating by the creaking of the wire by which it was pulled, now ceased, to the great relief of all present, and they proceeded to mount the winding stone

stairs which led to their respective seats in
the gallery.   The Ardvoira pew was the
largest, that property being the most exten-
sive in the parish ; it was the front seat in
the middle gallery directly facing the pulpit.
The right-hand gallery belonged to Glen
Torran, and the left to Loch Voira.   The
pew was fitted up with large old-fashioned
chairs with wooden backs and arms, and had
lately been furnished with hassocks ; the desk
in front was hung with crimson cloth.   The
pulpit had been left as it was, and had a
heavy wooden canopy, but the roof of the
church had been lined with dark wood, and
ornamented with rafters, and the walls, which
had formerly been whitewashed, were now
painted a dull brick-red.   The stained
window, which for some weeks had been
the wonder of the neighbourhood, some of
the congregation regarding it with admiration, others with disapproval, had been put
up by old Mrs. Macdonald to the memory of
her husband.   It represented Abraham about
to offer up his son Isaac in sacrifice ; the

altar occupied the centre of the window, at
one side stood Abraham with uplifted knife,
at the other side was a ram of ferocious
appearance, which to those uninstructed in
the Scripture narrative would seem about to
butt the patriarch, the thicket in which it was
caught by the horns being in a manner left to
the imagination.

Many eyes were turned to the Ardvoira
pew as Lady Eleanor took her place. She
always walked in first and occupied the end
seat, a position she was wont to complain of,
'because if I should turn faint'—she would
say—'than which nothing could be more
likely, how is one to get out?' Yet she
never accepted the well-meant offers of her
friends to change seats with her, preferring to
fortify herself with a fan and a bottle of
strong smelling-salts. Next to Lady Eleanor
sat Blanche, then Elsie; next to her Mr.
Fitzgerald, armed with plaid and air-cushion,
Heathfield and Charles Hargrave; while in
the opposite corner, several chairs off, Lionel
sat alone. He had a fancy for that far

corner, observing that he liked to have plenty of room for his legs.

And now the minister ascended the pulpit stairs and was shut in by the beadle. Mr. Duff was fair, florid, and rather stout, with a good-humoured, but not very intellectual countenance; his voice was good, but his delivery somewhat pompous.

'Let us begin the public worship of God by singing to His praise part of the eighty-fourth Psalm. To the tune of Ballerma.'

He slowly read it over, and the congregation rose; for the custom of standing to sing, and kneeling to pray, had lately been introduced at Loch Voira church. The familiar words, and something in the plaintive sweetness of the tune, sent a thrill to Elsie's heart.

> ' How lovely is thy dwelling-place,
>   O Lord of hosts, to me !
> The tabernacles of thy grace
>   How pleasant, Lord, they be !
> My thirsty soul longs veh'mently,
>   Yea faints, thy courts to see :
> My very heart and flesh cry out,
>   O living God, for thee.'

The psalm was a favourite of hers, and
she remembered the last time (how long
ago it seemed!) that she had heard it in
the parish church of St. Ethernans.

Blanche was silent during the first verse,
but surely she too liked the music, or she
would not have joined in so vigorously with
her strong contralto, while Lionel from his
distant corner sent forth his deep bass notes
with evident satisfaction.

Then followed the long extempore prayer,
appointed by the Church of Scotland in her
dread of a written liturgy, but of which each
minister has his own particular form of words,
as familiar to his hearers as though they held
the prayer-book in their hands. First came
the ascription of praise to Almighty God,
dwelling on high above all heavens, amidst
light unapproachable, inaccessible, yet holding in His hands the life of every created
thing. Then the confession of our own low
and lost estate, the utter abjectness of which
was particularly insisted upon by this divine.
We were worms of the dust, cumberers of

the ground; our spiritual nature was full of wounds and bruises and putrefying sores; we might call corruption mother and the worm our sister; we had rolled sin like a sweet morsel under our tongue, and had drunk iniquity like water. Could we realise the full extent of our vileness we should lay our hands upon our mouths, and our mouths in the dust, crying, 'Unclean, unclean.'

He next dwelt at some length upon the 'scheme of salvation,' devised by the Almighty for our redemption from the slavery of Satan and the corruptions of our own hearts. Then a thanksgiving that this congregation had not been brought up in Popery or infidelity, but had their birth in this favoured Protestant land, which was illuminated by the pure light of the Gospel teaching. A petition that they might not be deemed unworthy of these high privileges, nor be led to engage in the services of the sanctuary in a spirit of carnality and formality, but that, putting the shoes from

off their feet, they might hear the Word
with reverence and godly fear, and that
the preaching of the same might be good
to the use of edifying, and might minister
grace unto the hearers, closed the exercise;
which was followed by the reading of a
chapter from the Old and another from the
New Testament.   After that a hymn and
a short prayer; then came the sermon.

'You will find the subject of the following
remarks,' said the preacher, 'in the fifty-
fifth Psalm, sixth and following verses: "Oh
that I had wings like a dove! for then would
I fly away, and be at rest.   Lo, then would I
wander far off, and remain in the wilderness.
I would hasten my escape from the windy
storm and tempest."'

The occupants of the Ardvoira pew had
listened to the opening services with various
feelings.   Lady Eleanor, who, it is to be
feared, was a little apt to be bored by any
church service, even the most ornate, but
who made a duty of going to church, and
behaving properly when there, settled her-

self back in her chair with an air of edifying resignation.   Blanche had very soon decided in her own mind that the minister was not worth listening to, and did not listen accordingly.   Lionel frowned, he did not like this style, and resolved to give his vote against the election.   Elsie, who had been stirred and moved by the singing, was disappointed ; she hoped a little from the text, which was rather an unusual one for a sermon, and which found an echo in her own soul ; but what views could that comfortable, well-fed unimaginative-looking pastor have about it ? They proved to have at least the merit of originality, and he began by gently blaming the Psalmist for his imprudent and ill-considered desire.

First he 'would direct his hearers' attention to the thing wished for ; the instruments by which David desired to accomplish his flight.   Wings have been, by the Divine Providence, denied to man.   There have been those who, in various ages of the world, have rashly attempted to soar upon pinions

of their own construction, and falling head-
long, have reaped, in contusions and broken
limbs, the consequences of their presump-
tuous act.   In these attempts we may re-
cognise a fitting type of those who, trusting
in their own strength, make to themselves
refuges of lies, and put confidence in vain
fables.   Let us seek to cast from us all the
appliances of merely human wisdom, not
trusting in an arm of flesh, still less in a
wing of feathers.

'But the aspiration of the Psalmist was
confined to words: "Oh that I had wings
like a dove!"   Nor, excepting for this, did
he suffer any murmur of discontent to pass
his lips.   How many men in his circumstances would have sought to engage in
unwarrantable strife and bloodshed, or at
the least have given utterance to unseemly
imprecations!   Such, however, is not the
language of our text.   The Psalmist merely
exclaims, "Oh that I had wings!"   Had
that rash desire been granted him — had
David been endowed with the wings of a

dove, and been enabled, by their assistance, to wing his flight into the wilderness—what the better would he have been? Where, we may well ask, would have been the satisfaction of that?'

The preacher proceeded, in the second place, to consider the wilderness or desert mentioned in the text. 'Commentators,' he observed, 'are not agreed as to the exact geographical position of the region to which the King of Israel desired to effect a retreat. Some writers suppose it to have been the desert of Sahara; others contend that the Psalmist, unacquainted as he probably was with the interior of Africa, would rather have sought refuge in the stony districts of Arabia, or in the wilderness of Sinai, in which his own forefathers had wandered for forty years.' These surmises, however, the minister allowed, were immaterial, and he passed on to describe a wilderness as 'an arid waste of sand, probably destitute of vegetation, resounding with the cries of savage beasts, and abounding with serpents and scorpions of the most venomous description. Exposed to the attacks of these ravenous creatures, and without the means of supporting life, we cannot be led to suppose that David would have been truly happy. Still,' the minister argued, 'if the circumstances in which the Psalmist was placed were attentively considered, it would be found that his wish to escape into the wilderness was not so ill-judged as it at first sight might appear to be. Absalom, from whose rebellious and unfilial conduct David desired to escape, was equally to be dreaded with the lion or the unicorn of the desert; while the treacherous and insidious counsels of Ahithophel contained poison not less deadly than the fangs of the cockatrice or adder.'

He then branched off into an account of the revolt of Absalom, which occupied a considerable time, and which he satisfactorily proved to have been typical of most of the occurrences recorded in the New Testament, as well as applicable to the state of our own hearts at the present day. Returning to the subject of his text, the preacher remarked in conclusion :—' First, how wrong it is to indulge in unreasonable desires, or to seek another sphere than that in which we have been placed by Providence ; and secondly, that, the world having been appointed to our first parents as a place of toil, we ought to desire rather to labour in the sweat of our brow '—here the minister wiped his forehead —' than idly to seek repose.' He then summed up his discourse by observing that ' we must beware of permitting ourselves to form harsh judgments of the conduct of others ; seeing that even the Psalmist's desire for the wings of a dove, though vain and futile, might, if carefully sifted, be found to contain some grains of that solid wisdom and judgment with which we should all earnestly seek to be endued.'

The sermon ended, the minister gave out an anthem, which was sung but indifferently, the choir not having had much practice in this kind of sacred music. It was followed by the long and comprehensive intercessory prayer. The minister prayed for the Queen : that her horn might be exalted as the horn of an unicorn ; that she might be anointed with fresh oil ; that her crown might flourish upon her head, and that the shadow thereof might fill the land. For the Prince and Princess of Wales, and all the other members of the Royal House. For all those who are placed in authority under the Queen, and over us : that they might be a terror to evil-doers and a praise and protection to such as do well. For the minister of this parish : that he might be blessed in his sitting down and in his rising up; that he might renew his strength like an eagle ; that his feet might become like hinds' feet ; and that he might long be spared to come in and to go out before this people. For those in the eldership ; for the poor and needy ; for those in comfortable circumstances ; for the rich, who should remember that to whom much is given, of them the more shall justly be required. For the heathen : that the

Gospel might be preached in all lands, and might cover the earth as the waters cover the channel of the deep. For the ancient people of Israel : that when the fulness of the nations is brought in, they might lift up a standard in the midst of them. For the sick and afflicted : that they might have the oil of joy for mourning, the garment of praise for the spirit of heaviness. For those stretched upon beds of languishing : that they should be caused to rejoice greatly, and to sing aloud upon their beds ; and for all those whom the restraints of Providence that day kept absent from the gates of Zion. Finally, for the assembled congregation : that a blessing might rest upon the services in which they had that day been engaged ; that they might prove to them a foretaste of the joys they should hereafter experience ; that they might be assisted in singing the concluding hymn of praise, dismissed with the Divine blessing, and conducted in safety to their respective places of abode.

To conclude the service, the second Paraphrase was sung, to the tune of Salzburg.

Those who had come to church with any
devout feelings had mostly, by this time,
sunk into a state of apathy. This was partly
Elsie's case; she had come oppressed and
anxious, hoping vaguely for something which
might direct and comfort her, or at any rate
raise her thoughts to a higher level; and
though she saw at once that the preacher
was formal and commonplace, she yet listened
eagerly for some little word of cheering,
some suggestion of the hoped-for rest.
When the minister complacently informed
his hearers that we were not idly to seek
repose, Elsie did not, like Blanche, feel
tempted to smile. She felt so tired, she
bent her head, and could almost have cried
with disappointment. The beautiful closing
paraphrase was more soothing, and helped
to quiet her irritated nerves. She stood
merely listening, until near the end, then
suddenly raising her head, she joined in with
a good heart at the words,

'O spread Thy cov'ring wings around,
   Till all our wand'rings cease,
And at our Father's lov'd abode
   Our souls arrive in peace.'

As they came out of church, Elsie felt her hand warmly grasped by Mrs. Carmichael, who was close behind. 'My dear, now see that you drive home, like a sensible girl,' said that lady. 'These long trails will just be the death of you.' Then, in a lowered tone, 'Heard ye ever such a rigmarole of nonsense? Now James will be ill-pleased at me if I don't ask the minister to dinner; I wish he would come to church himself, and he would maybe not be so keen to have the minister asked. But I must go, or I'll not catch him, stupid ass!'

'Blanche, shall we drive home?' said Elsie.

'Certainly, drive home,' said Lady Eleanor, overhearing her. 'Get in at once, both of you. Well, what did you think of the service?'

'The singing is wonderfully good for a

country church,' said Blanche. 'But, mercy
upon us! what rubbish the man did talk!
Elsie, what do you say?'

'Yes,' said Elsie, sighing. 'I don't suppose there is any harm in him, but he is a
thoroughly stupid man, and he will never
improve, he is so self-satisfied. There are
many such—but I hope they will not elect
him.'

'Oh yes, they will,' said Blanche. 'A
man like that is sure to be a Conservative;
he is so pleased with everything as it is, and
you will see Lionel will pine to have him.'

'Well, why not?' said Lady Eleanor.
'A good, respectable, pious creature, I have
no doubt.'

'I am glad Constance did not come,' said
Blanche. 'She would have been shocked,
and that is so tiresome.'

'She would have been shocked at the
wrong thing,' said Elsie, 'at his accent and
manner, and way of conducting the service,
which is not the thing which is of consequence.'

'As to the sermon,' said Blanche, 'it is, after all, not greater nonsense than I have often heard from the pulpit in England. I think sermons are a mistake altogether; at least, they always rouse my worst feelings.'

'You ought to be ashamed of yourself, then, Blanche,' said Lady Eleanor severely, 'and I wonder that you girls can permit yourselves to talk on sacred subjects with so little sense of—of how you ought to talk. It does not seem to me that you have any principle, either of you.'

'Perhaps not I, Aunt Eleanor, but don't scold Elsie; she is a perfect mass of principle.'

'I cannot, for my part, see that she is a mass of anything,' said Lady Eleanor; 'pray do not let me hear such expressions.'

'Young ladies,' observed Mr. Fitzgerald, 'are fond of indulging in exaggerated language.'

'I have not heard your opinion of the sermon,' said Blanche, regarding her uncle and aunt with a look of innocent inquiry.

But Lady Eleanor, who had not listened

to one word of the discourse, declined to commit herself in any way, and declared that she would have no more discussion upon the subject, since it was conducted in such an unbecoming spirit.

CHAPTER VIII.

'I could not see, for blinding tears,
The glories of the west ;
A heavenly music filled mine ears,
A heavenly peace my breast.
"Come unto Me—come unto Me,
All ye that labour, unto Me,
Ye heavy laden, come to Me,
And I will give you rest." '

IT was the custom at Ardvoira on Sunday to have tea in the drawing-room instead of in the library, and at an earlier hour, as the party had necessarily partaken of a light and early luncheon, to suit the hour of service.

Lionel did not appear until tea-time, and came in at last, saying, 'I have been making inquiries about the election, and I do not think we are likely to have Mr. Duff. The old people object to him, as they cannot understand his Gaelic—he is a Lowlander born, of course. I shall try and get in Macdougall, that little man we heard two Sundays ago.'

'Oh yes, Lionel,' said Elsie eagerly, ' I liked that little man very much——' She stopped abruptly, wishing she had not spoken, as she caught sight of Lionel's look of pleasure at the personal interest she seemed to take in the parish.

Blanche, who had left the room a few minutes before, now reappeared in her walking things.

'Why, Blanche,' said Elsie, ' I thought you were tired. Are you going for another walk?'

'To be sure,' answered Blanche. 'Remember that we must not "idly seek repose." I wonder if Mr. Duff walks for the benefit of his figure; he would if he were wise.'

'We had better all go for a walk,' said Lady Eleanor rising, 'and Blanche, I wish you would not be so flippant.'

Elsie did not feel inclined to go out with the others. The exertions of the last few days had really tired her, and she felt that she would be glad of a little quiet; so, taking a book, she withdrew to the library, and seated herself by the west window.

She had not been long there when Lionel came in. He took a turn through the room, as if half undecided, then went to the piano and began to play. Elsie was occupied with her own thoughts, and did not at first observe the restlessness expressed in his whole manner. A volume of Newman's sermons lay upon her knee, but she was not reading; her clasped hands rested on the open book, and her sad eyes were fixed upon the distant peaks of Jura, which looked faint and ghostlike in the soft autumnal light.

Lionel sat and played, pausing from time to time. From his seat at the piano he could just see the outline of her cheek, and her shining plaits of hair; her face was turned from him, and her thoughts were far away. He felt that he scarcely dared to speak to her; yet he must give some expression to the passionate yearning love which filled his soul, and he played Schumann's 'Liebeslied.' Elsie turned her head, and listened with a sort of wonder on her face; she had never heard him play so beautifully. Suddenly he broke into a strain so loud and wild and thrilling that it startled her entirely out of her dream, and filled her with a vague fear. It was Liszt's transcription of the 'Erlkönig'; Elsie knew it well, and the words almost seemed to haunt her. She rose, and, drawn by a power she could not resist, went and stood nearer to the piano. Lionel's face, lit up as it was with excitement, was so beautiful as he played, that she could not turn away her gaze from it; his dark eyes were filled with a strange fire. As she drew near he stopped abruptly and came towards her; something in his look frightened her, and she half put out her trembling hand to keep him back.

'Do not stop, Lionel,' she said, 'go on playing, but not that—something softer. Play "Auf dem Wasser zu singen," or that "Abends," by Raff, which you played the other night.'

'No, Elsie, I cannot; there is something I *must* say to you.'

'What have you to say to me, Lionel?' said Elsie sternly, her very fear giving her a desperate courage.

She stood before him, tall and pale, looking straight into his eyes as if to quench the passionate fire in them with the grave proud calmness of her own.

'Is it about New Zealand—that you will give up that foolish plan? O Lionel!' and her tone changed to pleading—'say it is that you have come to tell me.'

'It is not that,' said Lionel; 'listen—no, Elsie, you *shall* listen to me; I have kept silence for years, and now I must speak. You know what I have got to say; you have known it all along. You know that I have loved you from the first day I saw you. Tell me how much longer I must wait. It *must* be that you will care for me some time.'

'Never, never!' cried Elsie, bursting into tears. 'Oh, Lionel, my boy, I do care for you, but not—not like that.'

'It is a sin,' said Lionel, beginning to
stride about the room in his anger. 'Why
will you waste your love upon the dead,
who neither know nor care, when there is
a living——'

Elsie had turned from him, and covered
her face.

'I have hurt you,' said Lionel, 'I am a
brute beast. I will go away and never
annoy you any more. Say one word to
me, Elsie, before I go.'

'Lionel,' said Elsie, calming herself, and
lifting her head, 'I want you to understand.
Whether the dead know about us or not'
—her voice trembled, but she controlled
herself by an effort—'we cannot tell—very
likely not. But I gave myself to David—
not for this life only, but for ever, and I
will not change or be untrue to him because he is dead. I will love you, dear
Lionel, like a sister—more than any sister,
but you must never speak to me again like
this.'

'And is that your last word to me then,'

said Lionel somewhat bitterly, 'after I have waited years for a little hope? Elsie, your heart must be like a piece of stone!'

'I have only been a misery to you,' said Elsie, her voice failing again, 'but I did not mean it. I ought never to have come to this place.'

Lionel walked to the window, and stood there looking out, then he came back to her.

'I am going,' he said; 'I will vex you no more, Elsie. But do you not think that in time—a long time——'

Elsie shook her head. 'I would if I could,' she sobbed, and stretched out her hands to him. 'Oh, dear Lionel! I would if I could.'

He took her hands gently in his, stooped down and kissed her, and was gone; and Elsie, laying her head on the chair, cried bitterly and without restraint.

She did not know how long she had crouched there, when voices and steps on the gravel outside warned her that the walking party had returned. She started up, and mechanically pushing back her ruffled hair, withdrew into the shadow, and waited until the steps had passed the library door, then darted into the passage. She dared not go to her room for fear of meeting Blanche, the open air was her only refuge; so putting on a little gray cap which lay in the entrance-hall (it happened to be Lionel's), she opened the door softly, and fled like a hunted hare towards the shore.

That she must get away, leave Ardvoira at once, was her one thought—yet whither could she go? Her father forbade her to come to Rossie; Aunt Grizel in her feeble state was scarcely fit to receive a sudden visitor; and she was most unwilling to return to England without visiting her home.

These thoughts passed quickly through her mind as she hurried towards the sea, not caring where she went if only she could leave some of her pain behind, while strangely the words she had heard in church rang in her ears and mingled with her thoughts. 'Oh that I had wings like a dove! for then would I fly away and be at rest. Lo, then would I wander far off, and remain in the wilderness. I would *hasten* my escape from the windy storm and tempest.'

Elsie spoke the last words aloud; she had by this time reached the rocks, whose sharp black points stretched out far into the water, for the tide was going out. She never paused to take breath, but hastened on, springing from one rock, slippery with sea-weed, to another, till she saw that the pools at her feet were crimson, and the whole sky and sea and land were lighted up with the glory of the sunset. Then she stopped and looked out towards the west. The sun was sinking behind the distant islands, and the sky above was crimson, speckled with purple clouds. She stood and gazed until the sun's last spark had gone down behind the sharp rocky hills of Jura, and a fiery orange glow had come into its place, giving a new splendour to

the sky.   Before the solemn grandeur of
the sunset Elsie lost sight for the moment
of her trouble; it came before her like a
reproof for making so much of her own
petty griefs; and life and its sorrows seemed
like shadows, to vanish in the light of the
world to come.   She sat down upon the
rock and did not stir till the crimson over-
head had faded into orange, and the orange
into a tender green, while the fiery light in
the west had deepened into a dull red glow,
like the heart of a dying fire.   Then a
moaning sound was heard far out at sea,
for heavy gray clouds came driving up,
and a chill wind began to blow.

Elsie shivered, and rose with difficulty,
for her limbs were cramped, but a sense
of peace and a new courage had come back
to her heart.   She began to make her way
back to the house, thinking over what had
happened and what would be best to do.
That she must leave Ardvoira, and at once,
was certain; she would even, perhaps, no
longer be welcome there, for not only had

she lost Lionel for the present, as a friend and companion, but had, too probably, hopelessly estranged Lady Eleanor's affection.   It was impossible, Elsie knew, to keep her in ignorance of what had occurred, and she would almost certainly be deeply hurt and indignant on her boy's account.

Elsie resolved to write a note asking her Aunt Grizel to receive her the next night (a telegram, she knew, would startle the old lady as much as a sudden arrival), and find some means of getting it despatched early the following morning ; and she herself would start for St. Ethernans later in the day, although she would thus have to spend the night somewhere *en route*.

It was very dark when she reached the house ; she had to feel for the door-handle, which her chilled hands could scarcely turn. She went in, and toiled wearily upstairs to her own room, where a bright fire was burning.   A letter on the mantelpiece caught her eye ; she took it up, a little surprised, as letters were not usually received at Ardvoira on Sunday. It was addressed in Euphemia's straggling handwriting, and ran as follows:—

'ROSSIE, *September* 30*th*.

'DEAR ELSIE—I was not able to send Word sooner about little Peter in answer to your kind Inquiry for we have been that taken up owing to little Allan having likewise got the fever too. The Doctor said to get a Nurse to them and we got one from Edinburgh and thought her a Superior Person but yesterday the Captain found her in that State he just took and sent her away Immediate and the Doctor said to get another but the Captain will not for he thinks they are all likely given to their Bottle. My hands are terribly full for Agnes cannot leave Granny she is now entirely Bedrid and my dear Elsie if you would come and help me with the little Boys I would be very Thankful and the Captain I have not told him but he would not say a Word once you are in the House for he is extraordinary taken up with you and I would not ask you to leave your Grand

Friends but that you said you would like to come to Rossie and what will I do if little Allan is taken from me for he is far worse with the Complaint than Peter. Hoping you are quite well—I remain yours affectionately,

'E. Ross.'

Here was an end to all Elsie's difficulties at once.

Poor Euphemia! poor little boys! Of course she would go to Rossie; and she began hastily to consider how soon she could start on her journey. When the dressing-gong sounded, and the housemaid entered with the hot water, Elsie questioned her eagerly.

'Barbara, how did the letters come to-day?'

'Please, ma'am, Chonnee Gillies was coming from Portarnish, and he would caal at the post-office,' was the reply. Young John Gillies was a grocer's apprentice in Portarnish, and occasionally paid his family a visit on Sundays.

'Oh, Barbara! please say I cannot come

down to dinner—I have had bad news from home; but you need not say that, Barbara, just say I have a headache.'

'Yes, ma'am,' said the girl in a subdued and awestruck tone. 'Please, ma'am, will you be taking any dinner?'

'No, I will have a cup of coffee later. And will you find out when the early steamer for Oban passes, and come and tell me?'

'Yes, ma'am,' said Barbara again. Her rosy face had lengthened considerably; she moved away softly, and shut the door after her with the elaborate caution which she considered that Elsie's grief-stricken appearance demanded.

Elsie began to put together a few of the things she would require for her journey. 'Perhaps,' thought she, 'Lady Eleanor need not, after all, be told about Lionel; this call is quite a sufficient reason for my leaving at once. Shall I go and speak to her now?' and she glanced at herself in the glass. 'No! I will wait till after dinner.'

Barbara by and by returned with some

coffee, and the information that the steamer going to Oban might be expected to pass Ardvoira Point between four and five in the morning. She begged to know if she could do anything for Elsie.

'No, Barbara, thank you; I am going by the steamer, as my little brother is very ill, but I must speak to Lady Eleanor first.'

'It is a peety,' said Barbara sympathetically; adding with indignation, 'Chon Gillies was thinking he was fery clever pringing the post letters on the Saabath; but he might have let them abee whatever if he was to pring the pad news.'

Elsie had nearly finished her preparations, and was thinking how she could bring about an interview with her hostess, when a tap was heard at the door, and Lady Eleanor entered hastily.

'Elsie, what is all this, and what has become of Li——' she stopped as her eye fell upon Elsie's open trunk.

'Oh! Lady Eleanor, I have heard from Euphemia—my little brothers are both ill,

and they need me at home. I was coming
to tell you, only——'

'At home?' repeated Lady Eleanor—'at
Rossie? Absurd! I will not hear of it.
But pray where is Lionel gone? for that is
what I came to ask you.'

'Lionel!' exclaimed Elsie, seized with a
sudden terror, and putting her hand upon the
table for support—'I—I don't know. Was
he not at dinner?'

Lady Eleanor eyed her with great
astonishment, not unmixed with indignation.
'Elsie,' she said, moving forward so as to
get a full view of the girl's face—'I insist
upon knowing the meaning of this, Lionel
has gone to Portarnish, leaving no compre-
hensible message, and I desire you to tell me
what has happened, as I see by your manner
that you know perfectly well. And what in
the world are you crying about, child?'

'Oh! Lady Eleanor, I never dreamt of
Lionel going away—but he will come back—
you must send for him. I am the one who
should go, and you see I—I am just packing

up   It is dreadful—it is not to be borne, that Lionel should go away because of me.'

'Do try to talk like a rational being, Elsie,' said Lady Eleanor impatiently. 'Lionel has proposed to you, I imagine —well, what was your answer?'

'I cannot marry Lionel,' said Elsie in a low voice; 'he knows that. I am very, very sorry that he should care about me in that way.'

'You refused him?'

'What else could I do?' said Elsie despairingly.

There was a short pause.

'Well,' said Lady Eleanor with great and marked coldness, 'I cannot insist on your marrying my son. This is not what I expected from you, or hoped, but you are free to do as you like of course. I think it a little odd, that is all;' and she moved as if to leave the room, then breaking into a sudden sob, she cried out, 'You have driven away my boy, and I shall *never* see him again.'

'No, no, hush!' cried Elsie eagerly, 'do

not say such things. He will come back—
you must send for him—you must telegraph.
Where has he gone ?'

'To Australia, I suppose, where he has
always threatened to go—to the farthest off
place he can find. He will not come back
for my sending, girl.'

'He will, if you tell him I am not here.
Besides, he can't have gone to Australia
without his luggage,' said Elsie, practical
even in her excitement ; 'at any rate he can't
have gone far yet. How and when did he
go ? And what message did he leave ?'

To this Lady Eleanor replied that she had
not seen him herself, but had been told that
about six o'clock, when the letters came from
Portarnish, Lionel, after receiving his, had
ordered the dogcart to be got ready, and his
portmanteau to be packed, and had started,
leaving a message with the servants that he
was going to sleep at the inn at Portarnish
that night, and take the early steamer to
Glasgow in the morning.

It was not without difficulty that Elsie

elicited this information, which somewhat tranquillised her mind; though she was still nervously anxious that Lionel should be sent for home.

'Then, Lady Eleanor, perhaps he has had some business letter, he *may* not have left on my account. But telegraph to him—to the house of his man of business, and say I am gone to Rossie. That will bring him back.'

'But how can I let you go to Rossie when it is not safe? No, Lionel will never come back; you have driven him away, and there is an end of it.'

'Listen, Lady Eleanor. In any case I must go to Rossie; so, why not send the telegram, which will certainly bring Lionel back to you? It is quite necessary that I should go to help my stepmother. See! here is her letter—let me read it to you.'

'I can make no sense of it,' said Lady Eleanor, interrupting her when she had read a few sentences. 'I don't believe it is safe to let you go—I don't know what you want me to do—and what am I to say to Lionel?'

Elsie took a sheet of paper from her blotting-book, and wrote : 'Come back at once ; Elsie has been sent for home.'

'There,' she said, 'will not that do for the telegram ? Then my steamer will pass Ardvoira Point between four and five in the morning. May I have Duncan M'Intyre and the boat to go out to her ?'

'You confuse me so,' said Lady Eleanor. 'Are you sure that this—' holding out the sheet of paper—'will bring him back ?'

'It will certainly bring him, or else a letter from him,' replied Elsie confidently. 'And about the boat ?'

'You say your father wants you at home ? I do not understand——'

'Not my father'—hesitating—'my step-mother, but——'

'Read me the letter,' said Lady Eleanor very angrily.

Elsie did so.

'I do not think I can let you go.'

'Then you cannot send the telegram.'

They sat looking at each other for some

time in silence ; then Elsie came and knelt down beside her.

'You see, dear Lady Eleanor, you must let me go.'

And Lady Eleanor let her go.

CHAPTER IX.

'O dream of joy ! is this indeed
The lighthouse top I see ?
Is this the hill ? is this the kirk ?
Is this mine own countree ?'

ELSIE left Ardvoira in the gray light of the
early morning, and after a long wait upon
the rocks for the expected steamer—so long
that she began to despair of reaching Oban
in time to catch her train—she at last got
safely on board. There was no clear sunrise,
but a dull red light in the eastern sky, which
was piled with heavy gray clouds above,
seemed to threaten stormy weather, while
a cold whistling wind blew from the south-
east. After a long journey and many changes,
she at last reached the well-known Crossbriggs Junction, and took the coach for
Drumsheugh. The rain, which was only

threatening in the west coast, had come on in good earnest here—heavy dashing rain from the east, with fierce blasts of wind, and Elsie was fain to content herself with an inside place in the coach. It was four in the afternoon when it drew up at the door of the Ochil Arms, the principal inn in the village. Elsie noticed with annoyance that it appeared to be the scene of unusual excitement this afternoon, for she had counted on a quiet rest by the fire, and a cup of tea, before encountering the short but stormy ferry. The inn resounded with coarse voices, fiddling, and stamping of feet.

'Is there anything going on here?' she inquired of the coach driver as she paid his fare.

'Ou no,' replied the man; 'it's the feeing market in St. Ethernans the day, and a wheen fowks come ower here to hae a dance.'

'The feeing market,' thought Elsie; 'how unlucky!' She remembered that her father would never let her go near St. Ethernans on the occasion of this annual festival, which was attended by farm servants of both sexes, in order to be hired for the ensuing Martinmas term, and at which it appeared to be *de rigueur* that every one should be dead drunk. 'I shall never get a carriage in St. Ethernans,' she thought, 'the people will be too tipsy, and I do not think I could walk the three miles in the rain. I will hire a dogcart or something here, and drive across the moor it will not take me any longer after all.'

'Can I have a carriage to take me to Rossie at once?' she inquired of the land-lady, Mrs. Braid, a stout matron, whose flushed face and dishevelled headgear showed that she had been a sharer in all the excite-ment, if not in the actual revelry of the occasion.

'Rossie?' said the woman. 'It's a lang rod. Jock!' she shouted, addressing some one in the kitchen—'Can the leddy hae a machine to gang to Rossie?'

'Yas,' answered the invisible Jock laconic-ally.

'Awa' to the yaird then, and get it yokit.'

'Can I have a cup of tea?' asked Elsie, a
little doubtfully; 'or is the parlour full?'

'Ou, there's just twa-three gentlemen in
there wi' their drap toddy. Gang inower to
the fire, mem, or I mask the tea. Maggie!'
raising her voice, although the conversation
throughout had been conducted in a suffi-
ciently loud key—'*Maggie!* Here a leddy
seekin' tea. Deil's in the lassie, what's she
kecklin' at?' as shouts of laughter issued
from some back region. 'My word! but I'll
sort ye, ance I get a haud o' ye,' and she
departed in pursuit of her too mirthful hand-
maiden.

Elsie pushed open the parlour door, and
looked in; but the confined air, the fumes of
whisky, and the loud, rather quarrelsome talk
of the 'twa-three,' or, more accurately, nine
or ten 'gentlemen' therein assembled, caused
her to retreat quickly into the passage. She
sat down on the top of her box till the land-
lady reappeared.

'Mrs. Braid,' she said, 'I will not take

tea, thank you—I have changed my mind. Do you think they are getting the carriage?'

'Jock!' shouted Mrs. Braid, 'are ye no awa' yet?' She went away, and returned after a long, but apparently fruitless argument with Jock, who seemed to be half asleep, to assure Elsie, if she would 'just take a seat' in the parlour, the 'machine' would be forthcoming.

But Elsie was in no mood for patient waiting. She rose, and went herself into the inn-yard, where, to her great joy, she recognised one of the ostlers, a respectable-looking lad, who had once been a stable-boy at Rossie. She went up to him and addressed him by name, 'Andrew Wallace.'

The lad turned round quickly, and evidently knew her at once; but not deeming it consistent with etiquette to appear surprised, only touched his cap, saying respectfully, 'I hope you're well, ma'am.'

'Andrew,' said Elsie, 'could you drive me over the moor to Rossie? I want to go immediately.'

' I'll do that, ma'am, replied Andrew with alacrity. 'Will I get the dogcart?'

'Yes, please, anything—as soon as you can,' and Elsie returned to the inn, and resumed her seat upon her box till the dog-cart came round.

It awakened considerable excitement in the minds of the revellers, as well as in those of the street boys; and a crowd speedily collected at the inn door to witness the start, and make their comments thereupon. 'Aundry!' cried one. 'Eh! see at Aundry, awa' to drive the leddy!' 'A—ay! he's a pawky ane!' 'Dinna cowp her!' 'Nae faer o'm! wull ye gie's a ride ahent?' 'Come doun here, till I gie ye a SMAACK in the face!'

This last invitation, of which, as it may be supposed, Andrew did not hasten to avail himself, was given by an individual of peculiarly festive appearance, who reeled up to the dogcart, and seemed to be under the impression that he could climb into it back-wards; but Elsie and her box being now in

their places, Andrew drove off with all speed,
pursued by laughter, 'hurrays,' and shouts of
derision from the assembled crowd.

Elsie's relief was so great that at first she
scarcely felt the rain dashing in her face, or
the gusts of wind, against which it was hope-
less to hold up an umbrella. She drew the
hood of her mackintosh over her Sunday
bonnet, which she had resumed at the outset
of her journey, partly because it was the first
which came to hand, partly from a vague
impression that it gave her a somewhat
venerable appearance, and that it was more
seemly to undertake a journey, with a view
of nursing the sick, in a bonnet than in a
hat. As they ascended the hill, and reached
the high and bleak moorland district, she
began to feel thoroughly chilled ; her cheeks
smarted with the cutting rain, and the cold
wind felt all the more piercing after the soft
air of the West Coast. The horse stumbled,
shook its head, and in spite of pretty frequent applications of the whip, kept slacken-
ing its pace. Andrew got out to walk up

the long steep hill, and Elsie, in spite of his remonstrances, did the same.

'Poor beast! he is tired,' she said. 'Andrew, be sure you give him a feed when we get to Rossie, but do not come into the house yourself, for fear of spreading the fever; ask Mrs. Duncan at the farm to give you your tea.'

At length the long drive came to an end, and with a thrill of pleasure Elsie passed up the well-known avenue and reached the door of her home. Before she had time to enter, the Laird himself appeared on the threshold; and as Elsie hurried up the steps to meet him, he put out his arm with a wondering look, as if to prevent her coming nearer. 'Elsie! what—what are you doing here?' he said hoarsely. But Elsie was not to be repelled, she was too happy to be at home again; and, for the first time in her life, she threw her arms round his neck. 'Papa!' she cried with a low laugh of pleasure—'you will not turn me away from your own door?'

The Laird uttered a sort of grunt, but he

half returned his daughter's embrace, and almost lifted her into the house.

'You're—you're all wet,' he said, touching her shoulder gently with his hand.

'Papa, how is Allan?'

Her father stared at her, and then turned away.

'No chance for him,' said he—'no chance for either of them.   That doctor's a fool.'

'But little Peter,' said Elsie trembling, 'I thought he was much better?'

'Good Lord!' burst out the Laird, striking his forehead violently; 'what does it matter what he dies of? he's always sick. And you—you'll be the next one!' turning fiercely on his daughter.   'What, in the devil's name, brought you here?'

Elsie noticed with pain how changed and aged her father looked; how the lines on his face had deepened, and his limbs shrunk; he did not look half the size he used to be. She did not mind his rough reception of her, which was in truth rather affectionate than otherwise, and he was full of concern for her wet and cold condition. He took off her wet cloak himself, and would not permit her to go to Euphemia, who was in the sick-room, but desired the maid to prepare some food.

'I will go to the kitchen fire,' said Elsie, 'and speak to Marjorie.' As she went through the passage, the peculiar odour of the disinfectants sickened her a little, and made her realise more strongly the presence of illness, perhaps of coming death.

Marjorie hurried to meet her, for the news of Elsie's arrival had quickly spread through the house, and welcomed her with a trembling delight which she could hardly find words to express, and of which Elsie had scarcely believed the undemonstrative Marjorie capable.

'Eh! Miss Elsie, my puir lamb! siccan a night to come hame, and you just dreepin'! Eh, lassie! but I've wearied sair for ye,' and Marjorie wiped her eyes. 'Jessie, woman! put on a bit fire in the White room, and tak' down the sheets to get aired. Crater, ye'll

be stairvin,' she added, turning to Elsie, and
hastening her preparations for a substantial
tea.

'Oh, Marjorie! the poor little boys!'
said Elsie sorrowfully. 'Are they in great
danger?'

Marjorie looked at her in slight surprise.
'No the Peter one,' she said, turning a piece
of bread she was toasting upon her fork.
'He's comin' on fine, Miss Elsie; but he's
a weary bit thing, ye ken.'

'But Allan?' said Elsie breathlessly.

'Ay, he's been awfu' ill, but we're thinkin'
he's taen the turn; the doctor was rael weel
pleased wi' him the day.'

'Well, I'll go upstairs,' said Elsie.

But Marjorie earnestly entreated her not
to go to Euphemia until she had eaten. 'It
micht be your deith,' she said.

Elsie consented, and having changed her
dress, went to sit with her father until
Euphemia came down.

It was quite true that little Allan had
'taken the turn,' as the nurses phrased it,

and was on the fair way to recovery. Peter, too, was entirely convalescent, and able to sit up in bed, in his little red flannel gown, smiling, and hugging a black kitten, which had been brought in for his amusement. Elsie went to see the children, but was too worn out that evening to be of any assistance to her stepmother; the next morning, however, they shared the duties of the sickroom together. Euphemia had no turn for nursing; strange to say, it was her awkward sister Agnes who had always attended upon the aged grandmother; and Euphemia, active and housewifely as she was, was utterly helpless in cases of illness. Marjorie therefore had enjoyed the post of head-nurse up to the time of Elsie's arrival, and had ordered about her mistress in a way which was highly satisfactory to herself.

On the following day Allan was pronounced out of danger; all went well; and Elsie, in spite of the aching limbs which her wet drive and previous fatigues had given her, felt light-hearted and happy, as she had

never thought to be again. Euphemia was
very grateful and affectionate ; she shed
many tears, and poured out to her stepdaughter long histories of the children's illness and of her own anxieties and fears.

'Oh, Elsie! it's been an awful time! now
you've come we must hope the best, but I've
had like a warning not to rejoize too soon.
Hope the best and fear the worst, as Mr.
Souter always says—and oh! he's a godly
man !'

'How do you mean you have had a warning, Euphemia ?' asked Elsie, cutting short
the praises of Mr. Souter, the Free Kirk
minister, which she foresaw Euphemia was
about to pour forth.

'Oh, my dear, I thought that Allan would
maybe not take the fever at all, for he was
near a fortnight after Peter, and the doctor
he thought so too ; but oh, it's a dangerous
complaint! Peter he had it mildly, but
there's Angus Cameron lost two children,
and there's more cases about ; and here was
Allan just as ill as he could be. For three

nights that child was carried,[1] and he only
came to his right mind the day you came.
Me, I was near out of my judgment with
it all!'

'I wish I had come sooner,' said Elsie,
'but my father wrote so peremptorily——'

'Ay would he!' broke in Euphemia excitedly; 'he was that positive, he wouldn't
let me speak of sending for you; he said he
wouldn't have you brought here to your
death, and used words about it; but when
little Allan turned so ill, I thought he was
quieter like, and I just ventured; for you
know he had parted with the nurse at his
own hand, and he wouldn't get another, and
'deed I don't know that she was much use,
for she just drank even on, and snored so
that nobody could get any sleep; and so I
spoke to him at last, but he just raged on
me, so I took it upon myself, and you see
it's all for the best.'

'I saw by your letter,' said Elsie, 'that
you were dreadfully anxious about Allan, but

---

[1] Delirious.

I think we may really hope that he is quite out of danger now.'

'Oh, my dear,' said Euphemia, lifting her hands, 'the night I wrote to you I thought he was gone! I didn't know what to do, and I went for your father, and *he* thought he was gone; and oh! I thought if Mr. Souter was there to put up a prayer; but when I named it to your father he used words again, for he never will hear tell of the minister in the house, and him such a godly man. Eh! dear, dear!' and Euphemia sighed dismally.

In this manner did the afflicted mother relieve her overburdened heart, and Elsie listened to many tales of a like nature, until the conversation was interrupted by the Laird, who entered with the resolved step of one who has business on hand.

'I never heard such a chatterer as that woman is,' he remarked, eyeing his spouse grimly, but addressing no one in particular; 'she would talk your head off if you gave her time. Elsie, go you and put on your

things; I'm going to take you to St. Ethernans to see the old lady.'

'Oh!' said Elsie, rising doubtfully, 'I
should like that, papa, if——'

'I'm sure I don't know,' said Euphemia
plaintively. 'I daresay I'll manage; but
there's Peter to get his dinner, and he likes
Elsie to feed him, and——'

'I tell you I won't have her kept in the
house,' interrupted her husband. 'What's
the use of you if you can't feed your own
children? Elsie, the dogcart will be round
in five minutes—if you don't want to come
you can stay at home,' and the Laird, rather
offended, strode off, without waiting for an
answer.

In another quarter of an hour Elsie was
ready, and waiting in the hall; but neither
her father nor his dogcart had as yet made
their appearance. In course of time, however, the dogcart came round; and the
Laird, having ascertained, by putting his
head out of his room and feigning to look
for his boots behind the door, that his

daughter was ready, and appeared willing
and desirous to accompany him, at last
emerged, in high good-humour, and more
carefully dressed than usual.

It was a brilliant autumn day, with just
a tinge of sharpness in the air to make it
clear.   Elsie's spirits, which had been a
little depressed by Euphemia, rose as she
sprang into the seat beside her father; and
they drove off at a good pace.

'How nice everything looks!' she cried.
'Oh, papa! you have put up a wire fence
—it is a great improvement.   And this is
a new horse.'

'New!' said the Laird.   'I've had him
two years.'

'And I have been away five.'

'You're very fine,' observed the Laird
suddenly, looking at his daughter with some
complacency, and alluding to the neatly
fitting brown suit which she wore.

'Oh, this is nothing, papa,' said Elsie
gaily.   'You have no idea what a smart
and fashionable person I have become; but

I left my best clothes behind for fear they should catch scarlet fever.'

'Those people were civil to you, I suppose?' said the Laird, after a pause.

'Lady Eleanor you mean, and her people? oh, very, *very* kind.' She became suddenly grave, and was silent for a little, although they were now going slowly up the hill, and there was every facility for conversation. 'When I go back,' she was thinking, 'I shall find a letter from Lady Eleanor to say that Lionel has come back. There might be one by this time; and surely, surely it will come to-day. Why should I feel so happy unless some pleasant thing were coming?'

And now they reached the top of the hill; and there again was St. Ethernans, and the sea, and the blue line of hills that Elsie loved; and she remembered how she had sat and wept on that very spot, thinking she would never see them more.

'How foolish I was!' she thought. 'Never will I believe in presentiments

again!   Here I am at home, and at peace.
And what is to happen to me now?' was
her next thought, but she put it quickly
aside.   'I do not know, nor care.   Let me
be happy whilst I can—and be at rest.'

CHAPTER X.

'It is hard in this world not to dread meetings because of
partings ; greetings because of farewells.'

THE Laird had business in St. Ethernans
and at Nether Bogie which would detain
him some hours ; so he left his daughter at
Aunt Grizel's, promising to return for her.
Elizabeth's well-known face appeared at the
door, and she hastened to lead Elsie into the
parlour, where Aunt Grizel sat in her old
place by the fire. Nothing in the house
was altered, except Aunt Grizel herself, but
Elsie was saddened at seeing how feeble
and fragile-looking the old lady had become.
She was greatly agitated by the meeting
with her niece ; her voice was changed and
broken, and she had lost all her former
activity, being unable even to rise from her
chair without assistance.

Her mind, however, was as vigorous as ever, and it struck Elsie that either increasing infirmities had rendered the old lady more acrimonious, or else she was no longer restrained by her niece's youth from openly censuring her neighbours. As soon as she had recovered a little from the flutter of excitement into which she was thrown by Elsie's arrival, she began to reflect upon Lady Eleanor with some bitterness.

'What was the woman thinking of? has she no sense? To send a girl to nurse a case of scarlet fever — I never heard the like!'

'She did not send me, Aunt Grizel,' said Elsie, laughing. 'She advised me not. I wanted so much to come.'

'Then what was to hinder you coming before? That was your Aunt Caroline's doing, I suppose. Here's five years gone by, and she must needs wait till there is scarlet fever in the house before she could let you come.'

'Indeed, Aunt Grizel, she knew nothing

about the scarlet fever, so I really don't
think that can be laid to her charge. Aunt
Caroline has been very good to me,' she
added thoughtfully.

'So you never rued the day you went to
England?' said Aunt Grizel, looking at her
keenly. 'My poor bairn——'

Elsie came and sat on the floor in her old
way by Aunt Grizel's chair. 'No,' she said,
'I never rued it—I would not have been
without it.' After a pause she went on,
'Aunt Caroline would have let me come
home two years ago, but — I did not feel
then—as if I could.'

Aunt Grizel laid her hand softly upon
Elsie's bent head. 'That was a fine lad,
my dear,' she said.

'O Aunt Grizel!' cried the girl suddenly,
'speak to me about him! Nobody speaks
about him now; it is as if they had forgotten
he ever lived. You saw him that time; tell
me everything you can remember. I could
not have borne it then, but now — I just
weary for the sound of his name.'

Then followed a long conversation, in which Aunt Grizel narrated all she knew of David; his sayings and doings, and the impression he had made upon her. 'He minded me of his father,' she continued, 'in some ways; but he was darker—he'll have got that from the mother's side. I never saw her, you know; she was a beauty, and spoilt — as I've been told; but Archibald Lindsay was a real fine creature.'

'So is Lady Eleanor,' said Elsie eagerly. 'You would like her, Aunt Grizel, if you knew her.'

'Humph!' said Aunt Grizel, who evidently reserved her opinion upon that point.

'Papa never said anything, of course,' said Elsie, 'but—he liked him too, I think.'

'Yes, yes,' said Aunt Grizel; 'there's no doubt Robert took to the young man; it did him good to have a man body in the house. Robert's ill to please sometimes, and David must have been a good-hearted lad to cheer him up the way he did; for your father was like another being for the time.'

' I meant to ask you about papa,' said Elsie. 'He's surely not well, Aunt Grizel; his cheeks never used to have those deep lines in them, and he has lost his colour and grown thin.'

'Ah! well, it's partly acidity; and then Robert has a good deal to put up with—he that's always been used to have his own way.'

'He has that still,' said Elsie, looking troubled; 'at least Euphemia seems to yield to him in everything—a great deal too much, I should have thought.'

'Tuts!' said Aunt Grizel, 'she just puts me beyond patience! Those soft-headed, obstinate, peaky women are the worst to deal with; they yield, and then they go and take their own way. She's just wearing Robert —that's your father—to a thread; and he's never been the same man since you went away.'

'Do you think I ought to stay at home now? Aunt Grizel, advise me; and I will do whatever you say.'

'There's only one thing I would advise you now, and that is, to go home, and go to your bed,' said Aunt Grizel, looking at her anxiously. 'What in the world's keeping Robert? You're too white, child, and now —bless me! you're too red—you're all the colours of the rainbow!'

'I have got a cold,' said Elsie, laughing faintly. 'Don't be anxious, Aunt Grizel; you know I never take infection.'

'Humph!' said Aunt Grizel; 'I wish it may be so. Well, here's Robert at last.'

After the Laird came in there was no more talk of this sort, but the conversation turned on farming and the local news, and as soon as tea was over, Miss Grizel hurried them away.

'I shall come and see you on Sunday, Aunt Grizel,' said Elsie, as they rose to take leave.

'If the Lord will, my dear,' said the old lady solemnly; 'it's not for old people like me to look so far forward, for we know not what a day may bring forth.'

Elsie was subdued and quiet during the
drive home; somehow she began to feel less
certain about finding the letter; and she was
becoming painfully aware that she was very
tired, and that her throat was sore. 'Yes, I
have caught a little cold, papa,' she said, in
answer to a sudden question from her father;
'but it is nothing. I think I caught it the
day I came home, when it rained so hard.'

The Laird said no more, but touched his
horse with the whip and drove home very
fast. When they reached the door, he lifted
his daughter carefully down, and desired her,
in a severe tone, to go at once to her bed and
to put a worsted stocking round her throat.
Before going to her room, Elsie stopped to
look into the nursery. Euphemia came to
the door as she opened it. 'Allan's sleeping,'
she said in a whisper; 'he's coming on
nicely. Could you come to Peter, he's been
asking for you.'

'I will,' said Elsie rather wearily, 'but I
must change my dress first. Are there any
letters for me, Euphemia?'

'There's one sure enough; it'll be from the Drumsheugh people, for it's got a coronet and initials; I couldn't just make them out, but there was an I or a JY, and——'

'Well, I'll come back presently;' and Elsie went in search of her letter.

Euphemia was right; it was merely a note of kind inquiries from Lady Ochil, who durst not, for her children's sake, come to see Elsie in person. Elsie put it down, sick with disappointment. She sat down on a low chair beside the bed, and laid her weary head upon the pillow. Half an hour latter, Marjorie, coming in, found her in the same position, and, much alarmed, put her to bed without loss of time. Elsie scarcely spoke; she was faint and trembling, but when questioned, admitted that her throat was very sore.

All that night Marjorie watched beside Elsie's bed. She was undoubtedly attacked by some kind of fever, and became so rapidly and alarmingly worse that very early in the morning a messenger was despatched in haste to St. Ethernans for the doctor. When he came, his verdict was far from reassuring. He was a tall, grave, young man, who gave his opinion with the air of one whose words carry much weight ; but he was observed by those who knew him well to abstain as much as possible from giving any opinion whatever upon any subject.   He felt the patient's pulse, and took her temperature ; he fixed his solemn gaze upon her, first at one side, then at the other, then from the foot of the bed, and his face grew longer at each movement.   In answer to Euphemia's eager questions as to whether this was another case of scarlet fever, he only replied in a deep voice, ' There is grrate cause for aaprehension here.'

In solemn silence he wrote a prescription, then gave a few directions to Marjorie respecting the treatment of the patient ; and intimated that he would call again next day.

' Would you just step into the nursery while you're here, doctor ?' said Euphemia.

The doctor complied, and calmly surveyed

the two little convalescents, but without utter-
ing a word.

'What do you think, doctor?' asked
Euphemia, fluttered and frightened. 'Do
you think Allan not so well? He was a wee
bit fractious, but——'

'Here,' replied the doctor, 'is no longer
any cause for aanxietee.'

The oracle then departed, leaving Euphemia much impressed by his wisdom and
medical skill, which consoled her a little
under the new trouble of Elsie's illness.

'She is in the very best hands at any
rate,' thought she.

Marjorie, however, did not share Euphemia's cheerful view of the matter.

'I dinna ken what is wrang,' she said,
'but this is no the way Allan took it; an'
she'll need a heap o' care or she win roond.
I'll no leave her to the likes o' you,' she
muttered under her breath.

The Laird, restless with anxiety, made
frequent visits to his daughter's room to ask
her how she did, and to suggest remedies;

but Elsie took little notice, and scarcely seemed to know any one. Sometimes she would start up and ask eagerly, ' Has Lionel come back ? ' then, recognising Marjorie or Euphemia, would beg them to see whether there was a letter for her. She would always try to smile in answer to their soothing words, and lie still for a little while ; then the restlessness would return, and the same question be repeated.

The Laird began once more to turn his thoughts unwillingly towards getting a trained nurse ; but Marjorie, who had never left Elsie from the first, and was jealous of any one taking her place, remonstrated, and proposed instead to send for a certain Mrs. Dewar from St. Ethernans, who was Marjorie's cousin, and 'a rael purposelike woman,' and who could cook and superintend the housekeeping. That evening, therefore, found Mrs. Dewar installed, and Marjorie was left free to devote herself to her charge. Poor Euphemia, thus deprived of female companionship, was now thoroughly miser-

able, and it was well that her children took
up so much of her time and thoughts. She
would waylay her husband, and try to keep
him with her, but, though he was not without
a certain consideration for her, she entirely
failed to obtain from him either conversation
or sympathy, while Marjorie sternly, and
without the least ceremony, kept her out
of her stepdaughter's room.

There was no improvement in Elsie's
condition the following day; and on the
next, which was Saturday, the restlessness
had given place to stupor, and she lay apparently unconscious.

CHAPTER XI.

'Notre repentir n'est pas tant un regret du mal que nous avons fait, qu'une crainte de celui qui nous en peut arriver.'

WHILST these events were taking place at Rossie, Lady Eleanor was still waiting at Ardvoira for news of her son, and nearly a week had passed since she sent the telegram.

For the last few days Lady Eleanor had been irritable and uneasy. On reviewing the circumstances she did not seriously think that Lionel had gone to Australia; yet she was anxious about him, and impatiently longed for an answer to her message. On the other hand, she was dissatisfied with herself for having let Elsie go. She felt that it was not right, and it hurt her pride to make excuses for herself. If there was anything in the world that Lady Eleanor could

not bear, it was being found fault with ; even
the reproaches of her own conscience were
resented by her, but do what she would she
could not get rid of the accusing voice.

On the Saturday after Elsie's departure
Lady Eleanor received a letter from Lionel,
written from the house of an acquaintance in
Yorkshire, the brother of his New Zealand
friend. He wrote that business prevented
his immediate return in answer to her sum-
mons, but that he did not see why his
presence should be so urgently needed at
Ardvoira. Why had Elsie been summoned
to Rossie so suddenly ? He expected a
letter from his mother with distinct explana-
tions, and enclosed his full address. He
concluded by saying that he would come back
at once if she really needed him, and at all
events she might rely on his appearing at
Ardvoira in time to accompany her south.
It was characteristic of Lionel to add as a
postscript : ' I hope you have not been disturbing yourself about me all this time. I
wrote to you the day I left, on board the

steamer, but forgot to post it. Have just found the letter in my greatcoat pocket!'

Lady Eleanor was alone in the house that afternoon, all the rest of the party having gone off on a boating expedition; and she was seated at her writing-table, pondering over her answer to her son's letter, when a visitor was announced, and Mrs. Carmichael entered, looking somewhat disturbed in mind.

'Have you heard from Elsie since she left?' she inquired after the first words had passed.

'I had a note to tell of her arrival,' said Lady Eleanor indifferently. 'The child was better, I think she said.'

'I have just had a letter from my daughter Isabella,' said Mrs. Carmichael. 'Elsie is very ill.'

'What?' Lady Eleanor dropped the letter she held, and looked full at her visitor. 'You don't mean she has taken the fever?'

'My dear, I fear it is so. It is a great pity she went, never having had it, and I don't like the account.'

'And I let her go!' cried Lady Eleanor, rising and beginning to walk about the room. 'You are come to reproach me, I suppose— well, so will Lionel! You will all say it is my doing! and how could I help it? she would go.'

Mrs. Carmichael sat quietly and watched her. 'It was a pity,' she said again.

'Is she very ill?' demanded Lady Eleanor, stopping her walk. 'What does your daughter say?'

Mrs. Carmichael took a letter from her pocket, put on her spectacles deliberately, and read :—

'I met Dr. Robertson's carriage in St. Ethernans, and stopped him to ask for the Rossie children. They are better; but I was truly grieved to hear that dear Elsie has taken the fever. You know one can never get much out of Dr. Robertson, but he said there was considerable cause for apprehension. There seems to be no eruption, but sore throat and much fever. I wish they would get her a nurse, and better medical advice. We will send to inquire for her to-morrow, and will let you know the report.'

'You see,' said Mrs. Carmichael, folding up the letter, 'it is evident the girl is seriously ill. I wish I saw her father—I would give him a piece of my mind! It is a mad-like thing not to get a nurse, and I know what these St. Ethernans doctors are; this one is just a young ass, and the old one is quite dottled. It is a bad business altogether.'

'But she will get better? People generally recover from scarlet fever,' cried Lady Eleanor in great agitation. 'David and Lionel both had it—I have had it myself—it is not so very serious. Mrs. Carmichael, you don't think she is in danger?'

'I cannot tell,' said Mrs. Carmichael, 'but I don't like the account. However, I will let you know what I hear on Monday'—and she made a movement as if to rise.

'Stay,' said Lady Eleanor, 'do not go yet; let me think what can be done.'

'There is nothing you can do, except wait.'

'Tell me the truth!' cried Lady Eleanor; 'keep nothing from me — you don't think she will *die?* She cannot, it is impossible!'

Mrs. Carmichael laid a hand upon her arm. 'My dear, she is in God's hands.'

Then Lady Eleanor broke into sobs and tears. 'I see you think it. She will die— I know she will! and if she dies I shall never forgive myself! It was my doing— it was for Lionel. Oh! how could I let her go?'

Mrs. Carmichael stood astonished, and even a little shocked at this outburst of distress; she was accustomed to reserve, and could not understand or sympathise with such an open display of feeling.

'Hush, hush!' she said; 'don't put yourself into a state. We must not give up hope, you know; that would be quite wrong, and there is no reason for it.'

'I knew something was going to happen!' said Lady Eleanor. 'All last night I dreamt of David, and his face reproached me. Am I to lose Lionel and Elsie too ? Oh, surely it was a little thing I did to be so punished!'

'I do not understand,' said Mrs. Carmichael. 'My dear, tell me the whole story if it will ease your mind; but for any sake try to quiet yourself.'

Lady Eleanor turned abruptly to the window, as if not quite knowing whether to be offended or not, but the impulse to relieve her mind by speech overcame her; she turned round again with a hasty movement, and in doing so overset a vase of flowers which stood on the table. The water ran over upon the cloth, and trickled down upon the floor ; for the moment it arrested her attention, and she stood silently looking from it to Mrs. Carmichael with eyes which saw without comprehending. Her visitor replaced the vase.

'About Lionel, you were saying,' she said cheerfully, beginning to wipe up the water with her pocket-handkerchief.

This action recalled Lady Eleanor to her-

self. 'Never mind that!' she said with
irritation. 'Lionel asked Elsie to marry
him, as I daresay you have guessed.'

Mrs. Carmichael nodded. 'Yes, yes, I
thought as much.'

'And she refused him. I don't know
why,' she went on rapidly; 'I always thought
—but no matter. I was out at the time.
Lionel went away post-haste, without so
much as saying good-bye to his mother or
any one; and Elsie shut herself up in her
room, and said nothing to me—to be sure
she didn't know he was gone. When I went
to her in the evening to find out, and asked
her where he was, she looked perfectly terrified, and said she didn't know. Then, of
course, I found out she had refused him.'

'I am sorry to hear she refused Lionel,'
said Mrs. Carmichael in her calm voice.
'Do you think she knew her own mind?'

'Oh! I am sure I don't know. She must
have driven him to despair, poor boy, for he
was perfectly wrapped up in her. She was
frightened, as I said, when she heard he was

gone ; and I — I thought he would never come back, and I——'

'You fell foul of her, I suppose ?' suggested Mrs. Carmichael.

'Elsie had had a letter from her stepmother, wanting her to come home and nurse that child ; and she persuaded me to telegraph to Lionel that she was gone—she said that would bring him back. She was very urgent with me, and—well, I consented, and this is the end of it. She was off early the next morning.'

Mrs. Carmichael kept silence for a few moments, and Lady Eleanor still stood by the table, mechanically arranging the ornaments upon it. 'Of course you think I was very much to blame ?' she said.

'My dear, it is not for me to judge my neighbour,' answered Mrs. Carmichael gravely. 'We may all fall into mistakes, but we must just bear the consequences. I trust dear Elsie may get better yet ; we have no reason to think the contrary. I confess I didn't make the best of it to you, for I was a

kind of vexed with you, and my mind mis-
gave me for the poor motherless lassie. But
there is no use crying over spilt milk.'

Lady Eleanor's thoughts had begun to
wander during the latter part of this speech.

'How soon will the next report come?'
she asked abruptly.

'On Monday, I suppose; to-morrow is
Sunday. No! stop a minute—I will drive
to Portarnish to the English Church, and
call at the post-office for the letters. If
you come or send to Glen Torran in the
afternoon, you will get the news. Now I
must go.'

Lady Eleanor was uncommunicative to
her own party regarding Elsie's illness, and
cut their questionings rather short. In her
own mind she was planning what to do in
case no better accounts reached her from
Glen Torran. Elsie should not and must not
die, she said to herself. Such a thing was
impossible, unheard of; she would prevent
it. Mrs. Carmichael's words about the in-
sufficient medical attendance, which she had

scarcely heeded at the time, recurred to her;
and she made up her mind that she would
herself start for Rossie the first moment she
could—early on Monday morning. Lionel
should not have it in his power to reproach
her for what she had done; she would snatch
Elsie from the very jaws of death; she
would see Captain Ross and insist on pro-
curing the very best medical advice and
assistance. In the meantime she spoke of
this scheme to no one, not even to her
husband, but passed a sleepless night, re-
volving plans in her mind, and building
castles in the air, in which she saw Elsie
restored to health by her means, and happily
married to Lionel. The morning brought
a corresponding weight of anxiety and depression; Lady Eleanor rose with a headache, and found herself quite unfit to go to
church that day. Blanche, who was eager
to obtain news of Elsie's condition, begged
to be the one to go to Glen Torran, to which
her aunt consented, charging her to bring
back all particulars as speedily as possible.

She had not very long to wait; for Mrs.
Carmichael had made no attempt to detain
Blanche, and the girl, alarmed at what she
had heard, was in haste to upbraid her aunt
with what she thought her indifference.

'Aunt Eleanor,' she said, entering hastily,
'the accounts are no better, and I am sure
Mrs. Carmichael thinks Elsie dangerously
ill. You never told us she was very ill
at all.'

'I did!' said Lady Eleanor; 'if you don't
choose to listen, I can't help it. What did
she tell you to-day?'

'Only that she is no better, and they are
very anxious about her. That was all Lady
Ochil could hear. Aunt Eleanor, you don't
seem to care!' continued the excited girl.
'It is *dreadful* that we should know no more
than that. I want to go and nurse her, she
must not be left——'

'She is not going to be left,' interrupted
Lady Eleanor. 'Don't be so foolish, Blanche;
I am going to Rossie myself, and will see
that she is properly attended to.'

'*You*, Aunt Eleanor!' exclaimed Blanche
in great astonishment. 'I thought you didn't
like nursing—it would be much better for
me to go. What does Uncle Frederick
say ?'

'I have made up my mind,' said Lady
Eleanor; 'and I shall start to-morrow morning by the first steamer. Don't go talking
about it, Blanche; nobody knows yet;—but
I am certain they don't give that girl proper
medicines and things, else she would never
have been so ill.'

'I daresay not,' said Blanche, with her
air of superior knowledge. 'Country doctors
seldom understand the treatment of infectious
complaints. I think you are right to go,
Aunt Eleanor; still——'

'I shall leave everything in your charge,
Blanche. You have some sense if you
choose to use it—Constance has none. Now
mind you say nothing about it this evening.'

Mr. Fitzgerald was thrown into great consternation by his wife's sudden, and to him
incomprehensible design. He at first tried

to dissuade her by every possible argument, and finding this utterly useless, he consoled himself by looking out her trains in *Bradshaw*, and trying to prove that she could not reach Rossie under three days at the shortest. No sooner was this theory demolished than he received a fresh shock by finding that she proposed to go alone and unattended even by her maid ; but he insisted on sending his own servant, Pritchard, to see her safe to her journey's end.

CHAPTER XII.

THE next morning Lady Eleanor set off, on board the same steamer by which Elsie had left Ardvoira exactly a week before. Unlike Elsie, she got on board with little delay or trouble, but, owing to a stoppage of two hours at an intermediate port for the purpose of taking in sheep, the steamer arrived at Oban so late that Lady Eleanor missed her train. There was a later one, however, which was available, and, escorted by Pritchard, she succeeded, by six in the evening, in reaching Lauriston, a town a few miles from Crossbriggs Junction. Here, after hiring a carriage, she dismissed Pritchard, resolving to post the rest of the way ;

and, urging the driver to use what speed he could, she started alone upon her twenty-eight miles' drive.

Delays, however, were unavoidable; and the night had long since fallen when her carriage rolled up the Rossie avenue, and a sudden loud peal at the bell startled the watchers within the silent house. The children were asleep; Euphemia had quitted the nursery; fearful of disturbing her husband, and yet craving for companionship, she had gone to Marjorie's room, and the two were sitting over the fire, talking in subdued voices, Euphemia sobbing.

'Eh! Marjorie, this is an eerie house,' she was saying; 'you hear the queerest noises whiles. Last night I—gude sake, what's that?' as a second peal at the bell made both women start from their seats.

'It's the front door,' said Marjorie; 'it maun hae been the bell we heard afore. What's come o' the lassie that she disna gang till't?' and, taking a light, Marjorie hastened towards the kitchen. In the passage she met the Laird coming out of his room; he looked worn and haggard.

'Are none of you going to answer the bell?' he said.   'Can't you hear there is somebody at the door?'

'Yes, sir,' said Marjorie softly, and put her head into the kitchen, while her master retreated again into his room.   'Jessie!' she called in a loud whisper—'Jess! div ye no hear the bell? gang to the door, like a woman, for the Captain's rael ill-pleased.'

'I dinna like,' said Jessie, cowering and drawing nearer to Mrs. Dewar for protection.

'Tuts!' and without another word Marjorie turned her back upon the frightened girl and went to the door herself.   As she opened it, a tall lady in a long fur cloak came straight up the steps and into the house, as one who had a right to enter there.   Marjorie moved a little aside instinctively and said nothing, but held up her light to gaze with great wonder and fear in the face of the stranger.   She had never seen her before, this dark-haired,

beautiful, imperious woman ; what right
could she have there ?

Lady Eleanor looked beyond Marjorie
into the dark hall, as if expecting something, then turned and spoke to her.

'How is Miss Ross ?'

The candle Marjorie held wavered and
flickered in her trembling hand, and for the
moment no answer came.

'This is Captain Ross's house, is it not ?'
said Lady Eleanor, wondering at the look
of fear and perplexity in the woman's face.
'Will you take my card to your mistress ?'

'Yes, ma'am,' said Marjorie under her
breath, recovering herself now that she saw
she was speaking to a real lady of flesh and
blood ; 'but Captain Ross is in great trouble
this night, and—but will you please to step
in ?'

She led Lady Eleanor into the drawing-
room, where a dying fire still flickered ;
stirred the coals into a blaze, and left her.
For a moment Marjorie stopped outside
her master's door, fingering the card doubt-

fully, and half hoping he would come out and question her; but as there was no movement within, she was afraid to intrude, and took it to Mrs. Ross as she had been desired. She found her mistress in the nursery, sitting by little Allan's crib, and made a sign to her to come out; for poor Euphemia was treated with very little ceremony by her servants, and was herself inclined to behave to them as to equals.

Euphemia therefore rose with alacrity, and hastened into the passage, burning with curiosity.

'It's a strange leddy has come,' said Marjorie, 'and'—in an awestruck whisper —'she's speirin' for Miss Elsie.'

'And—and you told her?'

'No me!' said Marjorie. 'Here her caird—she bid me bring it to you. You'll need to gang till her, mem.'

'Lady Eleanor Fitzgerald,' read Euphemia. 'Preserve us all! Oh, mercy me, Marjorie! what'll we do? D'ye think she's come to stay?'

'Leddy Ailnor Fitzjairald,' repeated Marjorie. 'Aweel, mem, I dinna think she'll gang awa' the nicht. Will I mak' ready the best bedroom?'

'Stop, Marjorie! dinna go away,' cried Euphemia piteously. 'Oh, I don't think I can speak to her. What like is she?'

'She's a very grand leddy,' replied Marjorie. 'But gang you to the drawing-room, mem; it's doubtless your pairt to speak till her. Or speak to the Captain; I'se warrant *he'll* no be feared.'

'Oh, woman, come with me! I daren't walk the stairs alone.'

Marjorie followed in silence, with a certain contemptuous dignity, and they again paused before the door of the Laird's room. Euphemia knocked timidly, but no answer came. 'No, no!' she breathed out, arresting Marjorie's hand, which was raised to knock again—'he'll be angered—he heard well enough; I would rather face the lady.'

At the drawing-room door Marjorie stopped. 'Will it be your pleasure that I

bide here, mem?' she inquired stiffly.
Euphemia gave her a deprecating look.

'I'll not be long,' she stammered, fumb-
ling at the door, which was suddenly thrown
open from the inside, and she found herself
face to face with Lady Eleanor.

'Mrs. Ross? I am extremely sorry to
inconvenience you, but I was very anxious
about our dear Elsie, and I came—I trust
she is not worse?'

'Oh, my lady! oh dear, dear,' wailed
Euphemia, beginning to sob. 'Oh! what
will I do?'

'She is not—dead?' said Lady Eleanor
fiercely, making a step forward; then catching sight of Marjorie— 'What are you all
afraid of? why do you look at me so? what
do you mean? Take me to her room at
once; she will not die—she cannot be——'

'My leddy,' said Marjorie firmly, stepping
forward, 'Gin ye be come to see Miss Elsie
in life, ye're come ower late. She died at
six o' the clock yestere'en.'

Lady Eleanor was silent for a moment,

stunned; then threw up her clasped hands
with a wild gesture. 'Great God!' she
said — and turned upon poor helpless
Euphemia as if she would have slain her.
'Why did you not tell me, woman, that she
was dying?' she cried, stamping her foot.
'Why did you not write—telegraph? I
would have saved her—I came for that;
and you—you have been with her and let
her die before your eyes!'

Euphemia cowered and wrung her hands,
her sobs becoming almost hysterical.

'Whist!' said Marjorie, 'for the Lord's
sake whist! ye'll waken the bairns. My
leddy, Mrs. Ross is—is overcome, as you
see, and the Captain maunna be disturbed.'
She took Euphemia by the arm and drew
her away. The Laird was standing in his
doorway as they passed. 'Make less noise,'
he said gruffly; and was about to retreat
again when Marjorie stopped him.

'If you please, sir, Leddy Ailnor Fitzjairald is come, and she'll be seeking to see
you.'

'Come! where?'

'In the drawing-room, sir. She thought to see—she was not aware, sir, of the trouble.'

The Laird put his hand to his forehead.

'I cannot see her,' he said. 'Tell her so. Give her what she wants. What's the matter with *you?*'—turning to his wife—'that you can't attend to people?' Then, as Euphemia answered only by a still louder sob, he turned away with a weary impatient groan.

'Put your mistress to bed,' he said to Marjorie. 'Why do you let her overdo herself?'—He went back into his room and shut the door, then, as if by an afterthought, he put out his head again. 'See that you give that—that lady a civil message'—he paused, as if racking his brain to find one. 'Give her my compliments. If she will do me the favour to stay I will see her to-morrow.'

Marjorie had a hard task before her. Having attended to Euphemia, and provided for Lady Eleanor's accommodation, she returned to give the latter the Laird's message, and to conduct her to her room. Lady Eleanor was walking up and down the room, with clenched hands, in angry impatient grief; no longer the stately dignified lady Marjorie had met at the door, but a wild, passionate woman, with sharp, haggard face and disordered dress. Marjorie scarcely knew how to address her.

' If you please, my leddy,' she said, and stopped. No notice was taken, and she began again louder. ' The Captain, my leddy——'

Lady Eleanor ceased her fierce walk up and down, and made an impatient sign to her to go on.

' The Captain, my leddy,' said Marjorie, considerably embarrassed, looking down and plaiting her apron into little folds as she spoke, 'takes it very kind your being here, and his compliments, and he will hope to see you to-morrow. Your leddyship's room is ready,' she concluded, taking up the candle, and holding the door open for her to pass out.

Lady Eleanor went to the room prepared

for her without a word ; and Marjorie, having lighted her candles, said, 'The tea will be ready shortly. Will I bring it up ? or will your leddyship please to come down ?'

'I want nothing,' said Lady Eleanor harshly ; 'you can go. Please to leave me alone.'

Marjorie retired, and took counsel with herself as to what should be her next step. 'My certie, she's a proud leddy yon ; I'se warrant few would say nay to her. But to think as she could keep the puir lamb in life when it was the Lord's will that she suld dee. Eh ! it's an awfu' like pride yon. But for guidin' hersel' she's nae better nor a bairn. She maunna gang fastin' till her bed ; I'll tak' her up her drap tea.'

It was with no little trepidation that Marjorie again ventured to the best bedroom door with her tray ; but she was sustained by a sense of her own importance as well as of duty, and felt it necessary for the credit of the house that no visitor should be allowed to go 'fasting to her bed.'

Having knocked several times without
receiving any answer, she took courage and
went in.   Lady Eleanor had flung herself
upon the sofa with her head buried in the
cushions, and, overcome by fatigue and grief,
wept and moaned like a child, without restraint.   Marjorie waited till she was quieter,
then spoke to her soothingly, and tried to
raise the cushion under her head.   Lady
Eleanor made no resistance ; she seemed to
have no strength left to be angry or offended;
she drank the cup of tea which was held to
her lips, but pushed away all other food, and
Marjorie did not press it upon her.

After a while Marjorie offered to help her
to undress, but Lady Eleanor, still weeping
violently, shook her head.   ' Was it you,' she
said presently, ' who told me she was dead ?'

' It's ower true,' said Marjorie sadly ; ' but
oh ! my leddy, dinna greet that way.   It's
the Lord's will.   He kens best.'

' Best !' cried Lady Eleanor.   ' How dare
you say so ?   Why should she die ? she was
young and strong.   It is monstrous, it is

cruel. Why do you stand there? are you made of stone? have you no feeling? But you do not care, I suppose—why should you?'

'Me? I daurna greet!' replied Marjorie, with a tremble in her voice that was half anger. 'Should na the Lord tak' hame His ain? I've held her in these arms—she's been like a bairn to me—and there'll be mony a sair heart for her sake forbye yours and mine. But it's no when she's lying deid ben the house'—here the tears trickled down Marjorie's cheeks—'that sic words should be spoken. And if you saw her—would ye come and look on her, my leddy?'

Lady Eleanor turned away shuddering but suddenly seemed to change her mind. 'I will come,' she said.

It would be difficult to define her motive in thus acting; for she had a natural shrinking from death, and everything connected with it, and in a calmer moment would have done anything rather than face such a sight. Perhaps in the morbid state of her feelings

she wished to spare herself no additional
pang; perhaps she had some undefined
lingering hope that Elsie might not be
really dead after all.   She might have fallen
into some long faint or trance, such things
were not quite unheard of.   There might be
a possibility of her reviving; or were it not
so, surely the released spirit could not be so
far on its way (even this wild thought crossed
Lady Eleanor's mind) that it would not come
back at her bidding—at her entreaty.

It was with a strange feeling, as of one
who walks in a dream, that she followed
Marjorie up the steps and along the narrow
passage to the turret room where the dead
girl lay.

As she went along Marjorie muttered a
sort of apology for her arrangements, lest
her reverence for the dead might seem to
savour of superstition.   'It's the White
room,' she said, 'an' it's a far way off—an'
I just left a pair of waux candles burnin'—
an' the Drumsheugh folk they sent white
flowers.   It's a fulishness, but it's their gude

will, nae doot. And she aye liket flowers,
dear lamb.'

The room was dimly lighted by the
candles Marjorie had placed there; and
between the white curtains lay the form of
Elsie, still and beautiful, with Eucharis lilies
laid beside her on the bed.

Marjorie had judged rightly. When
Lady Eleanor left that calm presence, all
violent agitation was subdued; she became
reasonable and quiet, and suffered herself to
be undressed and put to bed.

She understood now; dimly and painfully
she comprehended. That white rigid form
was not Elsie; the spirit which used to
animate it was gone where no weak earthly
cry could reach it; and she felt as she stood
there that even if the words were put into
her mouth which had power to call Elsie
back to life, she would not dare to speak
them.

CHAPTER XIII.

'And you shall deal the funeral dole ;
  Ay, deal it, mother mine.
To weary body, and to heavy soul,
  The white bread and the wine. . . .
But deal not vengeance for the deed,
  And deal not for the crime ;
The body to its place, and the soul to Heaven's grace,
  And the rest in God's own time.'

THE promised interview with the Laird did not take place next day. Lady Eleanor was too unwell to leave her room, and it was only towards evening that she was able to get up and sit by the fire, wrapped in her dressing-gown. Euphemia, after her night's rest, had forgotten most of her tremors, and was even disposed rather to plume herself upon the fact that she entertained a lady of title under her roof. She was officious in her offers of assistance, and, with a little encouragement, would have been glad to pour out to her guest the whole painful history of the last week, down to its minutest detail.   But Lady Eleanor would none of her.

'You are very kind,' she said, closing her eyes languidly, 'but I would rather you did not sit with me.   I really need nothing.'

'I am sure,' said Euphemia, twisting her hands, 'your ladyship is very easily pleased. I am really happy to see you so composed-like.   But is there nothing you could take? I am sure anything in my power——'

'I should like to see the woman who came to me last night, if you don't mind,' said Lady Eleanor.

Euphemia retired rather crestfallen; she would so dearly have liked a little gossip; and she had got no conversation out of Marjorie, who had been very 'short,' as her mistress phrased it, all day, and anything but respectful, for it must be confessed that Marjorie was considerably uplifted in mind by her success of last night.

She waited upon Lady Eleanor as desired; and the latter, opening her large dark

eyes, regarded her fixedly. 'What is your
name ?' she said.

'Marjorie Hay, my leddy,' was the reply
with a curtsy; for there was something in
this lady's manner which compelled from
Marjorie the respect which she denied to
Euphemia.

'Sit down there,' said Lady Eleanor, indi-
cating a chair opposite to her; 'I wish to
speak to you. You were — Miss Ross's
nurse, you said.'

'I was, my leddy.' And, encouraged by
Lady Eleanor's questions and evident interest,
she went on to tell her of many things—of
Elsie's childhood, and the old days before
she left Rossie; of the blank her absence had
made, and how her father had grown old and
worn before his time. How he had cheered
up at her return that wet and stormy day the
week before; how sweetly she had attended
to him and nursed the children until the
fever struck her down; and of the last few
days of suffering. Of these there was little
to tell; the poor child had been mostly wan-

dering, and had not been able to speak much ; but Lady Eleanor heard with tears of her constant questions about Lionel, and her anxiety that he should come home.

'But after that day,' said Marjorie, 'she was real quiet ; and when she couldna speak she aye smiled.   I kent from the first how it would be,' she went on, lowering her voice. 'I had had a warnin'.'

Lady Eleanor looked inquiring.

'The day she turned ill, she gaed awa' to St. Ethernans wi' the Laird, an' they were gey late of comin' hame.   I was lookin' for them, an' I thocht to take a breath of caller air at the door.   The sun was goin' doun in a bonny sky, an' I saw a white doo——'

'A white doo ?'

'That's a dauve,' explained Marjorie, 'jist a white dauve, an' it cam' oot o' the wast straight afore my een, an' flew in at the White room window—ye never saw the like —an' I gaed in, an' I seekit every pairt—an' there was nae doo !   It was a warnin'.   D'ye believe in thae things ?'

'I don't know,' said Lady Eleanor, startled at the pointed question; 'you should ask a clergyman.   But what happened next?'

'As I was sayin',' resumed Marjorie, 'Miss Elsie never held up her head sin' that nicht, an' it was on the Sabbath at the same hour that she died.   Ye ken the White room window is to the west—an' the sun it was near doun, an' the sky was red, red wi' a bonny licht—an' she gar'd me turn her wi' her face to the west.   I thocht she was a wee thing better, an' I went to draw up a bit o' the blind, an' stude there a minute; an' when I turned again—I took a thocht to send for the Laird.   An' she was gone before he came.'

Marjorie said no more, but sat looking before her musing, while Lady Eleanor leaned back in her arm-chair with her eyes closed. She looked very pale and sad; her thick dark hair hung loose about her shoulders; her white hands lay listlessly upon her lap. She had lost much of the imperious manner which had awed Marjorie at first; yet the latter, as she looked at her, was struck afresh by her uncommon and refined beauty. After a little while Marjorie rose.

'Will your leddyship be needing onything further?' she inquired with deep respect.

'No, nothing, thank you. Stay a moment. When is the—the funeral?'

'On Thursday, my leddy, at one o'clock.'

It was a still October day when Elsie was laid to rest by her mother's side in the churchyard of St. Ethernans. Lady Eleanor had fully made up her mind to attend the funeral, and see the last of her whom she so deeply mourned. During the intervening day she did not leave her room, as she still felt weak and ill, and was anxious to keep all her strength for this effort. She knew it was not the usual custom in Scotland for women to attend funerals, but for this she did not care in the least. No argument of Euphemia or Marjorie had the least effect in deterring her; but she was finally induced to give up her purpose by a somewhat peremptory message from the Laird, who inti-

mated that on his return he would be glad
to see her, but in the meantime he would be
much obliged if she would stay at home.

As the afternoon drew on, she could no
longer bear the solitude of her own room,
but came down to the dreary drawing-room,
and sat there with Euphemia, silent and abstracted. The Laird's refusal to let her accompany him made Lady Eleanor very unhappy,
not that the sight of the grave would have
been anything but most painful to her, but
because she was morbidly desirous of inflict-
ing penance upon herself, by way of atoning
in some sort for her carelessness of Elsie
while she lived. At first her impulse had
been to confess it all to Captain Ross, and
so, if possible, ease her conscience of its
burden ; but how could she meet the be-
reaved father, returning from his child's new-
made grave, and tell him that, but for her
selfish negligence, that daughter might yet
have been alive and well ? She looked
across at Euphemia, who sat opposite to her,
black-robed and tearful, yet complacent, her

mind still running upon the dismal hospitalities of the occasion.

But Lady Eleanor had little insight into character, and in her softened and repentant state she pitied Euphemia. Presently a carriage drove up the avenue.

'There's the Captain come back, poor man,' said his wife with a sigh; 'he'll like to see you, my lady. Not that he's in any hurry,' she added with anxious politeness, 'just whenever it suits your ladyship's convenience. Shall I tell him you are ready?'

'Stay, Mrs. Ross,' said Lady Eleanor, rousing herself to prevent Euphemia leaving the room. 'I had something to say to you.'

Euphemia sat down again immediately, but her guest did not speak for some minutes.

'I was very rude to you the night I came,' she said at last abruptly.

'Oh no! my lady, I'm sure I never thought——' said Euphemia in great embarrassment.

'But I was very rude,' repeated Lady

Eleanor sharply. 'Why do I say rude? I was brutal. Do you know why?'—she rose excitedly and stood before Euphemia's chair. 'You told me Elsie was dead, and it was my fault.'

Euphemia, terrified and uncomprehending, burst into a flood of tears. 'Oh! my lady, I know,' she sobbed out, 'I know it was all my blame her coming here; but Allan was so ill, and I was *that* put about—and oh! I never thought to have it cast up to me again. The Captain, poor man, *he* never said a word; for when she turned so ill I couldn't hold my tongue, and I up and *told* him it was my blame, and he never raged nor nothing.'

Lady Eleanor looked at her perfectly astonished.

'Are you in your senses?' she said. 'I cannot think what you mean. I tell you it was my fault—I let Elsie come here when I knew there was infection.'

'Your fault! oh, my lady, it was *me!*—I wrote to her to come.'

'So you did!' said Lady Eleanor, remem-

bering this for the first time.   She paused a
moment, while it slowly dawned upon her
that this other mother had also sacrificed
Elsie for her own child's sake.   'We have
both been to blame,' she said gently, taking
Euphemia by the hand.   'Do not cry so—I
never meant to agitate you.   We have both
cause to be most unhappy.'

Lady Eleanor's sympathy had never before
been so fully awakened.   Remembering her
own agonies of remorseful pain, she judged
others by herself, and had no comprehension
of Euphemia's duller nature.   In her great
compassion she took the sobbing woman in
her arms.   'Do not cry,' she repeated.

It was perhaps well for Euphemia that
she was at this moment summoned to the
nursery, whither she retired with a lightened
heart, impressed with the idea that all blame
was now shifted from her shoulders to Lady
Eleanor's.

During her absence the Laird entered.
The black clothes which he wore that day
altered him strangely ; and even Lady

Eleanor, who had never seen him before, was struck by his worn unhappy look. His manner was gruff as usual, yet there was an odd sort of dignity about him as he advanced and greeted her.

'I'm sorry to hear you've been indisposed,' he said when the first words had passed. 'You have taken a great deal of trouble coming here.'

'My coming has proved quite useless, Captain Ross, and I fear inconvenient. Will you forgive my troubling you at such a time? I leave to-morrow.'

The Laird made her a bow. 'I can't ask you to stay longer at present,' said he. 'Another time—in summer, when the weather is good, I should be glad to see you. Though there is nothing to come for now.'

Lady Eleanor raised her head to frame some answer, but none came, her eyes were full of tears. The Laird too had evidently something to say which he had a difficulty in bringing out.

'I am obliged to you,' he said at length,

'for the regard you have shown to my daughter. She—she was very sensible of it.'

'She was very dear to me,' said Lady Eleanor in a broken voice.

At this moment Euphemia entered, and caught the last words. She saw Lady Eleanor standing before the Laird pale and agitated, and looked anxiously from one to the other. Nothing surely, short of his displeasure, could have brought tears to her ladyship's eyes. The foolish kindly creature felt impelled to interfere on her behalf, for terrified as Euphemia was of her husband, she never could let him alone.

'Oh! Captain, you'll surely not be ill at her ladyship, and her so kind as to take the blame on herself. For indeed, until her ladyship came I thought it was me that did all the mis—chief, but you see now that I am not so senseless as you make out.'

' I don't understand a word you say,' said the Laird. He fixed a stony stare upon his wife ; then looked inquiringly at Lady Eleanor.

'I had not intended to speak again on this most painful subject,' said the latter rather haughtily, but with her eyes on the ground. 'I left it to Mrs. Ross to tell you—if she wished it—at a better time; but I know too well that your present grief is greatly owing to my carelessness. I might have prevented her coming here. I have been much to blame.'

'There is no blame,' said the Laird sternly. 'I blame nobody. It was all a mistake together,' he added, putting his hand to his forehead with the weary gesture which had lately become habitual to him.

Then he turned upon his wife. 'Go to your children.' He said this with such bitter sharpness that Euphemia started aside as if he had struck her.

'Yes, yes,' she whimpered, 'dinna be put about now—oh, Captain, you're so hasty! and me just newly come down!'

'Would you—oblige me—by going to your children?' said the Laird with ironical politeness, holding the door open for her to pass out. When he had shut it after her he came back to Lady Eleanor, who had seated herself, and looked on at this little scene with a slight expression of contempt upon her face.

'My wife—means well,' he said. 'At least, I suppose so. She came to me with some story about a letter she had written— women can't hold their tongues—if she spoke of it to you——'

Lady Eleanor made an affirmative sign.

'I wish it to be understood that *I blame no one.*' The Laird said this with difficulty, as if putting some force upon himself, and choosing his words with great care.

'You are generous, Captain Ross,' said Lady Eleanor.

'While I am upon this subject—which need not be returned to'—he continued with the same laborious formality—'I have some things here which should belong to you.' He opened a desk which he had brought in with him, and placed in Lady Eleanor's hands a case containing David's watch and the ring which he had given to Elsie. Then, without giving her time to speak, he looked at the clock, and, muttering that he had some business to attend to which would detain him till dinner time, and that he would send down Euphemia, he hastily left the room.

Except at meals, and at the moment of her departure from Rossie the next day, Lady Eleanor saw no more of the Laird. He was polite to her, and behaved to his wife with studied gentleness, evidently putting some strong restraint upon himself.

As she drove away and left him standing upon the steps, something in his figure and look brought tears into her eyes. They never met again, but Lady Eleanor always speaks of the Laird of Rossie with deep regard, almost with reverence.

CONCLUSION.

THE foregoing record of events was written some years ago, and it was then necessary, for obvious reasons, to end the narrative somewhat abruptly, for it is impossible for the faithful chronicler to write an account of events before they have taken place.

But if the reader has any curiosity to follow the fortunes of the various persons who have figured in these pages up to the present time, he cannot do better than look into Rosamond Ponsonby's drawing-room on a November afternoon four years later, and listen to her impressions of her kindred and friends as she finds them on her return from abroad. For the Ponsonbys have wearied of wandering, for the present, and decided upon buying a house in London, and furnishing it at their leisure, which is likely to afford them agreeable occupation for a year or two, or until something more interesting turns up.

They have just returned to their new house for the winter, and Blanche Hargrave has come to pay her sister a visit, bringing with her her latest-born, the son and heir, whose arrival has lately so engrossed his mother's thoughts as to render her somewhat indifferent to all that has taken place outside her own immediate family circle.

Rosamond is as gay and bright as ever, and looks absurdly young to be the mother of a girl of fourteen; yet there is a trace of dissatisfaction on her face, as if she found life disappointing. Perhaps she is too ambitious to be a thoroughly happy woman; whereas Blanche, lying back on her sofa and pretending to knit a baby's sock, looks the picture of content. She has grown stout, too, and matronly, and looks about ten years older than Rose, whose conversation she finds frivolous, and to whom she is in the habit of giving sage advice as to the management of her husband and daughter.

'I have just come back from such a funny visit, Blanche,' said Rose, sitting down with her back to the fire, and disposing herself for conversation. 'To Chippingham of all places! Just fancy old Mrs. Lindsay asking *me* ! It was on William's account, of course—but, after all, we got on quite well together.'

'Who is old Mrs. Lindsay?' asked Blanche vacantly, 'and why shouldn't you get on together?'

'Blanche, do rouse yourself and pay attention,' answered Rose. 'I am in a mood for talking, and I insist on being listened to. I know you think of nothing, day and night, but those babies of yours; but you have not forgotten Elsie Ross, surely?'

'Is it likely,' said Blanche with dignity, 'when I have a little Elsie at home to remind me of her constantly? But I remember now about Mrs. Lindsay; poor Elsie used to talk of her often—go on, I am interested.'

'It is odd,' said Rose, pausing. 'I used

to wish to see it all so much, as Elsie described it. It is changed now, of course — the old General being dead; but Mrs Lindsay is much the same, I should think.'

' I didn't know the General was dead.'

'The old lady told me all about it. He died more than three years ago, not long after Elsie. I don't mean that her death had anything to do with his—he never heard of it even, being unconscious at the time. It was paralysis, as far as I could gather, but poor Mrs. Lindsay uses so many figures of speech.'

'Poor old lady! and how does she get on without him ?'

'Oh, she is happy, I think, in her own way. Yes, he is her sainted Henry now, you know ; and she visits his grave—it is always an object for a drive. And she keeps anniversaries—she put off our visit on account of some anniversary, because she cannot have any one staying in the house on these occasions. I am trying to remember which one it was—it was not the

day of his death—or of his birth—or of his
funeral—or of his paralytic stroke—or of
their marriage — I think it was the anniversary of the day on which he proposed
to her, but I am not sure. And she has
her dear Cecilia to live with her — Miss
Maynard—not a bit changed, I am certain;
and the self-same servants, Parkins and
Howell and Trotter; but there is no Her-
bert; the buttons boy has disappeared from
the establishment. There is still a footman
called William, though I think he must be
a different one; Mrs. Lindsay was always
saying "William!" in a severe tone, which
was very terrifying, for I thought she meant
my husband, and that he had been doing
something wrong; but he is as great a
favourite as ever, and she puts up with me
for his sake. There is only one pug now
—a very fat one called Bijou, with a most
repulsive expression. The old lady was
interested to hear that little Hans is still
alive, and that Mona loves him so. She
was fond of Elsie, I do think, in her own

way; but it would not have lasted; she is always setting up some new idol. At present it is one of the Ernest Maynard's children.'

'Oh yes,' said Blanche, 'I remember that name; Elsie mentioned it, and I made her tell me all about the engagement, for I was interested in engagements then. Describe Mr. Maynard, Rose.'

'I can't describe him, although I was taken to his house. Mrs. Lindsay said it would be so good for me to see the model of a happy English home. Mr. Maynard was there, certainly, the whole time,—a tall man with correct clothes and black mutton-chop whiskers,—and he opened the door for us and shut it again, and handed tea, and did everything he ought to do; but somehow he made no impression on me, he seemed entirely merged in his wife, whose flow of conversation never ceased. The children were brought in——'

'Are they fine children? how many?'

'Only two, and they are not so fat as

yours, Blanche, nor have they such big black eyes; but they are prodigies of beauty and intelligence, according to their mother and Mrs. Lindsay. Caroline Cecilia, who is three, can both say grace and repeat a hymn; and Henry Beauchamp Dale, at one and a quarter, is aware that he is his mamma's darling, and his papa's joy, and his Aunt Caroline's comfort, and his Aunt Cecilia's treasure. He can also blow a kiss to Dr. Barnardo. Mrs. Lindsay says of these children : " Lina's is a *sensitive, ethereal* nature, but of the two, Beauchamp has the more angelic disposition." He will often, his mother told us, take the sugar-plum from out of his own mouth to "pop" it into his sister's. By the bye, I don't remember ever seeing your Molly or Elsie doing that, Blanche. I am afraid they haven't a giving spirit.'

'What nonsense, Rose,' said Blanche impatiently. 'Do talk of something else. Have you seen Heathfield's bride ?'

'No,' was the answer, 'I only heard of

her from Aunt Eleanor, but she seems to be perfection. Well born, well brought up, well off, pretty—but not pretty enough to turn anybody's head, very amiable, just nineteen, Heathfield very much in love, and his parents in the seventh heaven of delight. Happy Heathfield! I wish '— here Rose's tone grew graver—'we could hear the same news of Lionel, poor dear boy.'

'You used not to like Lionel,' remarked Blanche. '*I* always did.'

'Well, I like him now,' said Rosamond. 'He is very much improved, and no one could help being sorry for him. He has gone through so much, and borne it so well; and he is so good to his mother, it is quite pretty to see them together. I wish he would marry, for his own sake; though it would be a terrible blow to Aunt Eleanor, of course.'

'Not a blow at all,' said Blanche. 'Aunt Eleanor is always wishing for his marriage; why, she says it is her chief desire on earth.'

'I know she *says* so; but I should be sorry for both her and her daughter-in-law if it came to pass. Aunt Eleanor will never take to any other girl as she did to Elsie— and no more will Lionel.'

'Do you think he will never marry, then?' said Blanche, sitting up on her sofa, and looking much concerned. 'What a pity! what a sad pity! Nobody to inherit all that money!'

'Lionel will never inherit the money, because Freddy will never die. I do not see how, humanly speaking, he ever can; he takes so much care of himself.'

'But then Lionel's children might get it— or grandchildren,' said Blanche, projecting her mind into futurity. 'People must think of those who are to come after them.'

'I do not think,' said Rosamond gravely, 'that Lionel will marry as long as his mother lives. He does not care enough about it to do anything that would annoy her. But if he lost her—and she looks so ill, Blanche, that I sometimes think she will not live long; she is terribly changed within the last year or two—then he would marry directly, for he is the kind of man who cannot get on without a woman in the house. And I think he would choose a good woman, and be happy —as happy as people generally are in this world; but he will never forget his first love.'

THE END.